HEIDI HEILIG

ON THIS
UNWORTHY
SCAFFOLD

 Greenwillow Books, *an Imprint of HarperCollins Publishers*

On This Unworthy Scaffold
Text copyright © 2021 by Heidi Heilig
Map illustrations copyright © 2021 by Maxime Plasse
Music for "The Lights of Lephare," "A Good Time," and "Leo's Song" copyright © 2021 by Mike Pettry; lyrics copyright © 2021 by Heidi Heilig. Reprinted by permission of the authors.

www.epicreads.com

The text of this book is set in Minion Pro. Book design by Sylvie Le Floc'h

Library of Congress Control Number: 2021933813

ISBN 978-0-06-265200-3 (hardcover)
21 22 23 24 25 PC/LSCH 10 9 8 7 6 5 4 3 2 1

First Edition

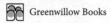 Greenwillow Books

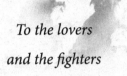

To the lovers

and the fighters

CAST OF CHARACTERS

The Chantray Family

Jetta Chantray. *A necromancer and shadow player.*

Akra Chantray. *Jetta's brother, who she brought back to life with her blood.*

Samrin Chantray. *Her adoptive father, whose stage career ended when the Aquitan questioneurs cut off his tongue.*

Meliss Chantray. *Her mother, a flautist and drummer.*

The Chakrans

Leo Rath. *Jetta's constant companion, a mixed-race violinist and half brother to Xavier and Theodora Legarde.*

Camreon Alendra, *also known as "The Tiger." The leader of the rebellion, and the rightful king of Chakrana.*

Raik Alendra. *The Boy King, Camreon's younger brother, put on the throne by the Aquitans.*

Cheeky Toi. *A showgirl turned rebel, and Leo's close friend.*

Tia LaLarge. *A singer and impersonator who joined the rebels with Cheeky.*

Le Trépas. *The necromancer who fought the Aquitans, using the souls of his own people.*

Ellisia Rose. *A madame favored by the Boy King.*

Ayla of the Ros Sook. *A shadow player who won recognition in the Fêtes des Ombres.*

The Aquitans

Theodora Legarde. *A famed beauty and inventor, engaged to Camreon Alendra.*

General Xavier Legarde. *The leader of the Aquitan armée, and brother to Leo and Theodora.*

Capitaine Audrinne. *A retired armée capitaine turned sugar baron.*

Madame Audrinne. *A rich patroness of Jetta's shadow-player troupe.*

Antoine "Le Fou." *The mad emperor of Aquitan, and Theodora's uncle.*

ACT 1

From: Antoine Le Fou, Roi d'Aquitan
To: Theodora Legarde

My dearest niece,

It was a relief to receive your letter, and to know you are alive. Good news out of Chakrana is in short supply these days. Between the rout of our armée from the northern jungle and the decree that all Aquitans are to be deported, it seems Chakrana is returning to the darkness from which we so long fought to save her.

As such, I was surprised by your plea that I throw our support behind this Camreon Alendra and acknowledge him as the rightful ruler—especially while the Boy King still occupies the throne. You claim this man is a long-lost prince, but there are no records of a prince by that name. Indeed, my own sources tell me that the only "Camreon" of note is better known as the Tiger—the leader of the rebellion that has been such a thorn in our side.

Theodora, you have lived in Chakrana long enough to know it is full of charlatans and opportunists. I hope you are not starting to believe them.

I cannot grant your request, but I have one of my own: come to Aquitan. Here you will be safe among your family, and you can turn your brilliant mind to more pressing issues than the tribalistic squabbling of a country fighting over scraps.

Are any of your marvelous flying machines still working? If so, I recommend you pack what you need and leave Chakrana. There is nothing left worth fighting for.

Your uncle,

Antoine Le Fou

Roi des Aquitains

CHAPTER ONE

It's been three weeks since my last dose of elixir, and despite all the warnings about my malheur creeping back, I've never felt more hopeful.

It might be the way the sun glimmers on the paddies, as though the farmers have planted diamonds instead of rice. Or perhaps the jubilant air of the crowd assembled in the field to watch the coronation.

It could simply be Leo standing at my side—or rather, at my ankle. I myself sit head and shoulders above the others, astride the living bones of the dragon animated by my blood. Still, if I leaned down, I could tousle Leo's dark hair;

he'd brushed it back so neatly for the occasion.

In the weeks since the battle at the temple of the Maiden, Leo and I have hardly been apart. In spite of the dead we burned and the wounds still healing, his steady presence is a comfort, and his music reminds me of good days gone by—and better yet to come. Now it's strange to see him without his violin in his hands. But of course our stage today is very different from the sort we're both used to.

We stand in a muddy paddy around the village of Malao, where thatched huts rise on bamboo stilts above the flood plain of the Riv Syr. It was Camreon's idea to resurrect the traditional rice-planting ceremony. His brother's coronation had been an Aquitan affair, but in the old days, the path to the throne started here.

Though the stage is humble, it is well set. Leo and I stand behind the king, and my brother Akra too—the Unkillable, the rebels call him, though not to his face. And of course Theodora Legarde, Leo's half-sister, fat and radiant in a dress fit for a future queen. Privately, the Aquitan beauty is still mourning her older brother, but you'd never know it by the smile on her face. It flickers only when she catches sight of Leo—after all, he is the one who shot General Xavier Legarde.

Camreon himself faces his people, ignoring the muddy water seeping up the hem of the traditional robe he's donned for the occasion. I'm used to him in stolen armée greens, but knowing Cam, there's a gun under all that silk.

"My ancestors stood in these fields," he's saying. "Planting rice as I do now. For a ruler must tend their country like a farmer tends their fields. Tireless. Vigilant. Nurturing." He smiles a little. "Unafraid to get their hands dirty."

The audience smiles along with him; many of them are farmers themselves, like most Chakrans outside the capital. The crowd is smaller than we'd hoped, but larger than we'd feared. And Malao is close to the Riv Syr, where news travels even faster than trade. The gossips will have plenty to talk about. Not least that the throne itself is still occupied by Camreon's younger brother, Raik.

Or rather, by Raik's body. I am not the only nécromancien in Chakrana.

If I close my eyes, I can still see Le Trépas's smile as he falls from the back of my dragon—down, down, down to the jungle far below. My fists clench, as though I could reach out and grab him back. It's my fault he's free. Raik may be the one who let him out of his cell, but I'm the one who let him fall into the jungle.

My brother's voice in my ear makes me jump. "That was your cue."

I glance across the stage, but Akra still stares, stone-faced, out at the audience. One of the side effects of my having raised him from the dead is that we can talk at a distance. I don't bother responding—all eyes are on me, and the only thing worse than missing a cue is for the audience to think I'm muttering to myself about it.

Hiding my embarrassment, I nudge my dragon forward. The floral garlands around her neck sway as she moves. Leaning down, I pass Camreon the ceremonial wooden bowl I've been holding. In it, three green shoots of rice wave like banners in the breeze.

"I have spent too much time with blood on my hands," Camreon continues smoothly as he turns back to the audience; he too knows the value of appearances. "But kings would do well to learn from farmers: we harvest what we sow."

A cheer goes up from the crowd; it's a good line. I myself have seen Camreon sow more corpses than seeds, but the moment the Aquitan armée began to retreat, the Tiger sheathed his claws, offering clemency for anyone who joined him. Not that many have; his reputation as a vicious killer, which served him so well during the rebellion, was proving a little more difficult for a king.

Still, he tucks each slip into the soft mud with the practiced hand of a man who has planted before. The audience looks on solemnly, but only I can see the souls that drift around the green shoots: the dead are watching too.

"For the Maiden," Camreon says. "For the Keeper. For the King."

The crowd stirs again—the older ones know their lines, and the younger ones echo as they learn. "For the living, for the learning, for the dead."

I speak the lines with the others, and they feel like a memory—or is it only the magic of theater? Around me, the souls swirl faster, as though they are caught up in the moment. But this time, I am ready—if I miss my second cue, Akra will never let me hear the end of it. Reaching into the little basket atop my dragon's neck, I lift out a dragon-bone crown.

It is even more finely carved than the one that vanished with Raik's body. My papa had spent the last three weeks working on it, and even though he lost some of his fingers to the Aquitans, it might be his finest work yet.

I hold it up, pleased to see the eyes of the audience

following. In a silence so deep I can hear the distant birds singing, I rest the crown on Camreon's brow. When the audience cheers, I hold back the urge to take a bow.

Tears spring to my eyes; applause always makes me emotional, and we had been planning this show for weeks. It is not the end of the fight, not with Raik and Le Trépas in control of the capital. But it feels like the start of something new. I wish my parents were here to see it, but they are still in the valley of the temple, safe in rebel territory. I'll have to try to capture it all in a letter: the cheering crowd, the king standing proudly in the mud . . . and Leo, smiling up at me.

"Nice prop work," he says, teasing, and at last I reach down to muss his hair. Laughing, he catches my arm and pulls me into a kiss. It is several moments before I realize the crowd has gone quiet. My dragon lifts her head sharply, turning her nose downwind. A man has stepped from the tree line, mounting the berm at the edge of the paddy . . . a soldier d'armée, with a rifle slung over his shoulder.

Could he be a deserter, come to join our cause? Then two more emerge from the jungle, a prisoner between them. The man's head hangs down, and his hands are tied in front of him. Even this far away, I can see the blood on the prisoner's shirt.

Anger flares in my heart. The armée was defeated at the battle of the temple. How dare these stragglers try to intimidate the rebel leader at his own coronation? Quickly the villagers start to disperse—old and young alike have seen this play out too many times. The swaggering soldiers, the Chakran prisoner, the accusations real or imagined—it would be a farce if it didn't always end in blood. But this time, I'm in a position to stop the show.

When I whisper to the dragon's soul, her bones uncoil beneath me. We stalk through the mud as the floral garlands sway.

"What are you doing?" Akra's voice is sharp, and I can't tell if he's shouting after me or if it's only in my head.

"I'm not missing another cue," I reply.

Leo calls after me too, but I pretend not to hear. Petals flutter behind us as I urge my dragon faster. I don't bother pulling the knife from my belt; the creature's teeth are twice as long as the blade. Instead, I crouch low over the bony spine, making a smaller target if the soldiers shoot. But as we draw near, their leader raises his empty hands in surrender.

"A truce!" he calls as his men follow suit. "We're not here to fight!"

For a moment, I wonder if I should pretend not to have

heard him either. Yet while the villagers have fled, I know Leo is watching. So I rein the dragon in, glaring at the men standing before me in the mud. Then I look at the prisoner and falter. The red stains on his shirt are crusted and old; he lifts his head, and his face is a gray ruin.

This man is already dead.

I suck air through my teeth, and the taste of rot tickles the back of my throat. I spit into the water, and the spirits of little fish scatter, shimmering. If they are near, then Le Trépas isn't—souls flee his presence, as well they should. But this walking corpse is the first sign I've seen of the old monk since his disappearance . . . at least, outside of my nightmares. My heart beats faster—not with fear, but with excitement. If Le Trépas has left the capital, it might be easier to track him down and kill him.

"You must be Jetta Chantray," the first soldier says, jolting me out of my reverie. His eyes flick between my face and the dragon's teeth. "The nécromancien."

"How did you guess?" I say wryly, but the soldier doesn't risk a smile. Though he looks too young for his rank, the epaulets on his shoulder gleam. "And your name, lieutenant?"

"Charles Fontaine," he replies crisply, his hands still in the air. "I'm hoping to speak to the king."

"You mean Camreon?" The question tumbles out of my mouth before I can stop it, and I can't hide my surprise: the armée backed Camreon's brother Raik for years.

"The very same," Fontaine says crisply. "Formerly known as the Tiger, and rightful heir to the kingdom of Chakrana. We came to ask his aid."

Suspicion creeps in. Chewing my lip, I glance over my shoulder. The Tiger is approaching, much more cautiously than I had. "With what?"

"This, to start with." Fontaine nods toward his prisoner. "I don't suppose it was your handiwork?"

My lip curls. "When *I* raise dead men, they heal."

"Le Trépas, then."

"It looks that way." Any soul that suffers a cruel death would become a n'akela; Le Trépas had made many in his time, including the spirits of his own children. A body occupied by a vengeful spirit had an icy-blue glow in their eyes, but this prisoner's eyes are a soup in their sockets, like cooked rice left for days in the bottom of a covered pot. He isn't even Chakran, I realize with a start. His matted hair is light brown under the soil and fluid, and his stained shirt was once armée green. Likely one of the soldiers that fell during the battle at the temple—but that's far west from here. "Where did you find him?"

"The plantations, just a few kilometers downriver," the lieutenant replies. "There have been several attacks on Aquitan civilians in the area."

My stomach clenches, queasy. When I was a shadow player, we performed in quite a few of the fine homes along the Riv Syr. Our best patrons, the Audrinnes, owned most of the land there. "Are there survivors?"

"If so, they've fled. Or been taken to the capital for deportation," the lieutenant says darkly.

"And the dead?" I press him. "Were the corpses all raised, like this one?"

"Many were," the lieutenant replies. He glances again at my dragon's teeth. "I must admit, I never would have believed it if I hadn't seen it with my own eyes. I was sure the old stories about nécromancy were just that: stories. But even stranger, all the dead we found carried the same message."

"A message?" I frown. "From who?"

"It isn't exactly signed," Fontaine says delicately, his hands still high in the air. "Do you want to see it?"

I open my mouth to answer, but Camreon has come up behind me on quiet feet. "Why don't you tell us what it says?" he calls from a distance, his gun pointed at the lieutenant.

"I can't." Fontaine wets his lips. "It's written in Old Chakran."

Cam raises a skeptical eyebrow, but a thrill goes through me at the thought. The language had been forbidden by the Aquitans—I had only just begun to learn it myself. The message must be from Le Trépas.

What could it say? Is it for me? I hear his voice sometimes, half in and half out of a dream. He teaches me like he used to, sharing his secrets—spells and magic—but when I wake, I can't remember the words.

"Show me," I say eagerly, and Fontaine lowers his hands. But rather than reaching into his pocket, he pulls back one half of the prisoner's shirt, like a bizarre sideshow curtain. The message is carved into the skin of the corpse's chest.

My stomach flips, but I cannot look away. Ragged wounds, black blood, bruised skin . . . on top, the symbol of the Tiger—four slashes, like claws. And below it, a deep V, like a book just cracked open, or a vessel ready to be filled. The Keeper, the third deity. "Knowledge," Camreon reads, shaking his head. "Less a message than mutilation."

"So it's meaningless?" the soldier says, and I slide from the dragon's back to get a closer look.

"The symbol usually has an accent," I explain to him, the way Camreon had so recently begun to teach me. "Depending on where it is, it changes the meaning."

"Not enough to matter," Cam calls, but I peer at the mottled torso, the mud sucking at my bare feet. "Stay back, Jetta!"

Rolling my eyes, I lift the other flap of the filthy shirt between the tips of my fingers. "He doesn't have a weapon, Cam."

"Anything can be a weapon," the Tiger retorts, but I ignore his warning. There, down low: a stab wound under the point of the V.

"'Know your enemy,'" I translate, with a sense of satisfaction—I don't know much old Chakran, but I've been studying. "It's part of the proverb. 'Know your enemy and know yourself, and you'll have nothing to fear.'"

"It doesn't matter," Cam snaps. "Come away!"

Annoyed, I take a breath to retort, just as the corpse wraps blue fingers around my wrist. Blinking, I pull back, but his grip is like a shackle. The dead man grins. Metal shines dully behind his yellow teeth. Someone has stuffed a grenade where his tongue used to be.

As the corpse pulls the pin with his free hand, the armée men scramble. A shot rings out; the body jerks, but bullets can't kill the dead.

Everyone is shouting, swearing. Leo calls my name as he races toward us. Frantically, I haul back, feet slipping in the mud; my heart pounds as I fumble for my knife. How much time do I have? Not long enough to cut myself free, but I don't need to. Sliding the blade across the tip of my finger, I mark a bloody new symbol on the corpse's own wrist: death. A flash of light—the soul flees—the bruised fingers go slack.

Suddenly off-balance, I topple into the paddy. Muddy water closes over my head. Gasping and coughing, I scramble to my feet. I can't see, but the smell of curdled blood fills my nose. Akra's voice echoes in my ears. "Run, Jetta!"

But which direction?

Wiping my face with my wet sleeve, I open my eyes just in time to see Fontaine throw himself over the corpse, pressing the body into the muck. The explosion throws gore and mud over me in a wave of wet heat. I stumble away with a splash, my ears ringing in the blast. As I sit, stunned, rain falls gently around me . . . not water, but blood.

FOR IMMEDIATE DISPERSAL

1er Octobre

By order of King Antoine of Aquitan, all officers are commanded to bring their remaining men to Nokhor Khat to assist in the deportation directives given by King Raik Alendra of Chakrana.

The *Prix de Guerre* shall be immediately supplied and outfitted to bring our people home at all speed. Gather your men at once and report to the docks in Nokhor Khat.

Capitaine Xavier Legarde

CHAPTER TWO

"**J**etta!" Leo's frantic voice is far off. Muffled. Dazed, I take a breath to shout back. Then I feel a hand on my shoulder. He's already at my side. "Are you all right?"

"I'm . . . fine," I murmur, though I can hardly believe it myself. Aside from the ringing in my ears and the nick on my finger, I am unhurt. If Le Trépas meant to kill me, he'd failed miserably. A wild laugh bubbles up my throat. One of the soldiers whips his head around at the sound, his face speckled with blood. The lieutenant's blood.

Fontaine is certainly dead, and the last soldier is wounded. As Leo helps me out of the mud, my heart races, my thoughts returning again and again to Fontaine's grim face as he shielded me from the blast. Why?

"What?" Leo eases me down on the dry berm, taking out a handkerchief to dab the mud from my eyes. I blink at him through the drifting souls as they cluster. They are drawn to my blood, so hungry for life. The lieutenant's soul is among them, a silent pillar of fire. Does he regret his sacrifice? "Why what?" Leo says again; only then do I realize I've spoken aloud.

"Why would he save me?" I say softly, passing a shaking hand through the golden light that is all that's left of Fontaine.

"Because he thought you could save us," one of the soldiers says through his teeth. With a grunt, he lays his companion down on the dry soil beside me. The man moans weakly, his left leg covered in blood.

"Any Aquitan who joins us has clemency," Camreon begins, but the first soldier whirls, his teeth bared.

"And what of the rest?" He wipes the blood from his face, his eyes wild, and suddenly I wonder what else the soldiers had seen at the plantation. "The ones who don't trust you, or don't know who the hell you are?"

"They're probably better off going back to Aquitan,"

Camreon says mildly, but the soldier laughs bitterly, looking back over the bloody water.

"Perhaps that's true," he says darkly. "But they'll be lucky if even half of them survive the journey."

Leo looks up from his fussing. "Why is that?"

"The *Prix de Guerre* is a cargo ship," the soldier replies. "She may be able to fit a thousand refugees, but not to feed them. I don't know what General Legarde is thinking."

At the name, Leo goes absolutely still, and my own heart stutters. The other soldier groans. "Teh-twa, Matthieu."

Matthieu ignores him. "No victuals, no medical. And low on coal, so the journey will take twice as long as it should!"

"General Legarde?" With needless care, Leo folds his filthy handkerchief. His voice is so quiet I can barely hear it—or is that only the ringing in my ears? "Are you certain?"

The soldier scoffs. "Who else would be giving orders that will get us all killed?"

The answer comes to me immediately: Le Trépas. But Leo is more circumspect. "I killed my brother in the battle of the valley," he says grimly. "Whoever is leading the armée now is not the same man."

Matthieu spits into the water. "Legarde might be a

terrible general, but I think even the officers would notice if he'd started rotting at his desk."

Leo stands abruptly, tucking his handkerchief into his pocket and starting off toward the thatched huts that rise on bamboo stilts above the flood plain. "I'll go get the docteur."

"I'll come," I say, starting after him, but Cam puts a heavy hand on my shoulder.

"Sit down till the docteur checks you for a concussion," he mutters. Then he raises his voice, calling after Leo. "Bring a cart and some shovels, as well! We'll bury what's left of Fontaine as honorably as we can. As for your surrender," he adds, turning to the soldier, "I accept. We need all the help we can get."

Gritting my teeth, I watch Leo trudge through the paddy alone. My heart tugs in my chest like it's trying to follow, but the guilt is a weight in my gut. I may not have resurrected Xavier Legarde myself, but it's my fault just the same. I failed to stop Le Trépas when I had the chance. Even worse, the nécromancien escaped with a vial of my own blood. We had hoped he'd only had enough to raise the Boy King, but it seems he raised the general as well.

Le Trépas told me once that the fighting wouldn't end until the Aquitans were all dead, but I was never foolish enough to believe him. Once they are gone, the old nécromancien will turn on the rest of us. "Know your enemy," he had written, and I do. Le Trépas is everyone's enemy.

I rub my wrist; I can still feel the corpse's cold fingers there. Had the monk killed the Audrinnes as well? The guilt grows, pressing me into the mud, but it's hard to imagine my old patrons dead or fleeing. Even during the famine of the Hungry Year, as the rebellion intensified, Madame's riches had helped shield her from the effects of the very war such wealth had caused.

My memories of performing shadow plays in her sitting room seem like a dream, vivid and nonsensical. Had I ever been a performer? An artist . . . a shadow player? The war has stripped away all the proof I'd had—our traveling roulotte, painted and carved, burned to ash. Our fantouches, some passed down from Papa's ancestors, all but one lost as well. Maman's instruments—the thom and the bird flute—left behind at Leo's theater in Luda as we fled. The theater itself too, the last place we'd performed . . . destroyed by the armée.

Suddenly I want, more than anything, to go back to Madame's sitting room. To find the makeshift stage she ordered built and rebuilt every year; to peek around the side of the white silk scrim to see the gilded chairs lined up along the polished wooden floor. To hear the polite murmur of the audience turn into an expectant hush as they wait for the show to begin. To light the lamps, to raise my hands, to make my shadows dance across the screen.

But if Le Trépas was there, the Audrinnes must be dead too. Or corpses, raised like the prisoner was.

Now the weight in my stomach turns to heat. I start to rise again, but Cam pushes me back down. "The docteur," he reminds me, but I'm tired of waiting.

"I'm fine!"

"You may be unhurt," the Tiger says quietly. "But you're far from fine. Leo's been watching you like a hawk, and you still almost managed to get yourself killed."

I blink at him. "He's what?"

"He's trying to keep you safe," Camreon says. "But he could use your help."

Taken aback, I stare after Leo, but he has vanished into the village. Was that why he hadn't left my side the last few weeks? All of his tender attention—his constant care . . . was it love or duty?

"I know I've been without my elixir," I say with careful calm. "And I know you're all worried about my malheur, but I also know my own mind, and I'm fine."

"I look forward to the docteur saying the same," Camreon says, and though it takes all the composure I can muster, I sit back down to wait.

When the docteur arrives at last, she treats the wounded soldier first, while Matthieu stares warily at the tattoos on her back. All of her sins, written on her skin in Old Chakran. She was a monk once. When the Aquitans were in power, she would have hidden the markings with long sleeves; the skin of her arms is still paler than the deep tan on her hands. Now she wears a Chakran sarong, and the light of the setting sun is like a blessing on her shoulders.

Once the soldier has been loaded into the waiting cart, she turns to me, peering into my eyes and running her hands across my scalp. "Any ringing in your ears?"

"No," I say—it's not exactly a lie. The ringing has faded into a thin whine. I could almost mistake it for a persistent mosquito. The docteur narrows her eyes.

"Watch for nausea and dizziness," she says. "But the real danger is a second blow to the head while you're recovering. You should rest for a few days, just in case."

I can feel Camreon's eyes on me, but I only grit my teeth. "I'll keep that in mind," I say. "Can I go?"

"Take the cart," Camreon interjects, and it isn't worth

it to argue. The wounded soldier and I trundle back to the village at the pace of the placid water buffalo, while Cam and Matthieu stay behind to bury Fontaine.

By the time we reach the village, the blood has dried on my skin, and flies are buzzing around me thicker than the souls. Leo is waiting for me in the village square, where preparations for a coronation feast are underway. "Are you all right?" he says, helping me down from the cart, and there's nothing I want more than to fall into his arms.

Instead, I hesitate. "Have you really been keeping an eye on me?"

"Of course I have," he replies easily. "It's impossible to look away."

The flattery makes me laugh, especially as I stand stinking in my filthy sarong, and just like that, I *am* all right. After all, Leo has known about my malheur from the start—perhaps love and duty are not always in opposition.

"Let's get you cleaned up, shall we?" He takes my hand, leading me toward the huts. The locals in Malao have welcomed us into their homes, giving Camreon the largest one, with three rooms separated by woven screens and curtained doors made of silk. The main area has been converted into a makeshift war room, with a map of Chakrana pinned to the wall and a scattering of soft pillows in the corners.

Miu lounges among them—the fantastical dragon fantouche I had ensouled with the spirit of a kitten, the only fantouche I have left. When I step up through the hatch, she bounds toward me to bat at the flies that have followed me inside.

Theodora's greeting is much less effusive. "I'll take it from here, Leonin."

She used to call him Leo, like I do; it was only their brother who called him by his full name. Leo doesn't bother correcting her. He only steps back, letting Le Fleur herd me toward the sleeping quarters, where Cheeky is waiting with a stack of towels, a pot of water, and a furious expression.

"Strip," she says flatly.

Peeling off my ruined outfit sarong, I give the showgirl a smile. "Shouldn't there be music?"

"Depends on what sound your head makes when I smack it," Cheeky growls. "What on earth were you thinking? We run *away* from grenades, not toward!"

"I didn't know there was a grenade at the time," I start, but she holds up a furious finger.

"You didn't know there wasn't! Throw that out the window," she adds as I try to find a place for the sarong. "It's unsalvageable."

"You should see the other guy," I say.

"I think I do," Cheeky says pointedly. "In your hair."

She wrinkles her nose as she picks something pink and gelatinous from my scalp. My stomach twists, and my smile falls away. "It's Le Trépas's fault," I say as Cheeky dips a towel in the water. "He's the one who sent the message."

"A little tip," Cheeky says as she wipes blood from my brow. "From someone more experienced with creepy old men. You don't have to accept every present they send."

Theodora folds her arms across her chest as Cheeky runs the cloth over my shoulders, muttering all the while. "Why did you get so close, Jetta?" Theodora asks. "Why did his message matter to you?"

I look at her, surprised—isn't it obvious to her? And if not, how can I possibly explain? The guilt I feel at his escape is a constant shadow—as is his lurking presence at the edge of my vision. Every time I close my eyes, I still see him falling, down, down, down. . . .

"Because I have to stop him," I say at last. Then I gasp as Cheeky pours water over my head—she hasn't bothered to warm it. The filth runs down my back in rivulets, dripping through the springy bamboo slats.

"Hard to do if you're dead," she says, and I snap.

"If I had died, I might have been spared this conversation!"

"If your own life doesn't matter to you, what about your brother's?" Cheeky's question stops me short—and now I know why she's so angry. "The minute you die, he does too. And what would your parents do then?"

"My parents?" The girl knows how to hit where it hurts. "That was low."

"My apologies for reminding you that you have responsibilities beyond Le Trépas," she says, with a smile like a knife. Her dark eyes flash as she dumps the rest of the water over the stains on the floor. "Try to remember it yourself next time."

Tossing the dirty towels in the basins, she carries it all out with a huff. My shoulders sag, the wind taken out of me, but Theodora isn't finished. "We're not strong enough yet to take the monk on face-to-face," she says, handing me a clean towel.

"So Camreon says." How many times have I heard this over the last three weeks? "But the longer we wait, the stronger Le Trépas gets."

"I don't think that's true," Theodora says mildly. "After all, the dead he raises don't heal like yours do. Corpses rot."

"He's more than happy making new ones," I mutter, scrubbing myself dry with the rough towel. "Besides, I've seen him rip spirits from their new lives with a drop of his blood and a bit of old bone. Now I know why it used to be customary to burn the dead," I add, tossing the towel into the corner and taking the fresh sarong she offers. "What could he do if he ever got hold of a lock of your hair?"

Theodora's hand goes to her own golden curls, and she wets her lips. But she doesn't back down. "I'm more concerned about what he'd do if he ever got hold of you," she says. "The rebellion relies on you, Jetta. On your fantouches—on your power. If you die, we lose our best weapon."

"I never wanted to be a weapon," I mutter as I wrap the sarong around my waist.

Theodora's face softens. I recognize the sadness there. After all, I had seen her inventions—the avions sketched by a girl who dreamed of flight, built by an armée for a nightmare war. "That's not all you are," she says, lifting my hair out of the way so I can tie the knot behind my neck. "You're a daughter. A performer. A friend." Her hands are gentle as she releases me. "Know your enemy, *and* know yourself, or so I'm told."

As she steps back, her eyes sparkle; I am the one who had told her that, months ago. And now Le Trépas is saying the same to me. "Thanks," I say, but before I can say more, Camreon's voice drifts through the screen.

"Can I come in?"

"We were just finished," Theodora says, sweeping aside the curtain as we return to the sitting room. Camreon breezes past us, pulling off his crown and struggling out of the muddy silk robe. "Are the soldiers settled in?"

"Just a minute." He returns a moment later, buttoning a fresh shirt over his silk binder. "I almost tripped half a dozen times in that robe. Worst way to die, facedown in the mud."

His look is pointed, but I wave him off as I take a seat beside Leo. Miu flicks her long tail in irritation at the disturbance. "Don't bother scolding me. Cheeky did a better job than you ever could."

"Practice makes perfect," Camreon replies with a faint smile. "Speaking of the soldiers, I found Fontaine's field orders. They were telling the truth. The armée is recalling all battalions to Nokhor Khat to help with the deportation.

The orders were signed by General Legarde."

At my side, Leo tenses, and his sister's face goes pale. But to my surprise, she nods. "It makes sense as a tactic," she says. "The Aquitans who might be willing to fight a decree from the Chakran king will have a harder time denying orders from their own armée."

"And of course, the *Prix de Guerre* is an armée ship," Camreon says. "The civilians won't know it's so ill-equipped for passengers. At least, not until they're aboard."

"The rest of the armée must know," I say. "Why would they go along with it?"

"They're used to following orders." My brother's voice precedes him up the ladder; he might be unkillable, but he isn't invincible, and he's still moving slowly after the battle at the valley. "No matter how terrible those orders are."

Hauling himself halfway into the room, he gives me a twisted smile as he sits on the edge of the hatch, one leg dangling through the opening. Another side effect of my bringing him back is his compulsion to obey any order I give him, in a way he never had to when he was in the armée. As such, I'm careful not to give commands—I don't even like to contradict him.

"Fontaine's own orders made reference to Le Roi Fou

sending supplies to stock the *Prix de Guerre*," Camreon says, but Theodora shakes her head.

"I doubt it's true," she says. "Even before the battle at the temple, my uncle was loath to spend more money on Chakrana. Besides, if he was sending supplies, why not send passenger ships?"

"Fontaine apparently felt the same," Camreon says. "Partially because he had come from Aquitan so recently. Apparently he was among the last recruits bound for Chakrana."

"I can fetch a bucket if we want to send him back," Akra says.

Leo looks at him, aghast. "We can't let the *Prix de Guerre* sail."

"Between the decree from the King of Chakrana and orders from the general d'armée, we don't have a choice," Akra says. "Unless you come up with the manpower to defeat the armée or take the throne."

"The manpower is already there," Camreon says slowly. "All we have to do is stop it from being loaded aboard the *Prix de Guerre*."

Akra's eyebrows shoot up. "You think the Aquitans will join the rebellion?"

"Some of us already have," Theodora says pointedly, but he waves the claim away.

"You knew Cam for years before you switched sides," Akra says. "The rest of the Aquitans think he's either a usurper or a murderer."

"They might change their minds if we save their lives," Camreon replies. "But we don't have much time. The *Prix de Guerre* leaves in three days."

"What about the Audrinnes?" I say then.

Camreon raises an eyebrow. "The what?"

"The Audrinnes." I stand, going to the window as Miu swirls around my feet, annoyed at losing access to my lap. Outside, the setting sun turns the sky bloodred; the river shimmers at the edge of the paddies, winding its way south to the sugar fields. "They own the plantation where Fontaine found Le Trépas's message. We should check there first. If we can catch the monk, there's no need to fight our way through Nokhor Khat."

"How so?" Theodora says, and I turn back, the excitement building in my chest.

"If Le Trépas dies, so do his minions," I say. "The Boy King and the general, not to mention any other revenants he's left in his wake. With the throne empty and the armée leaderless, you and Cam are clear to step into the breach and figure out what to do with the Aquitan civilians." I take a breath—the words are beginning to fall over one another. Then I look at Camreon askance. "Why are you shaking your head?"

"You assume Le Trépas will be easy to find," Cam says. "But why would he linger at the plantation?"

"What if he left clues behind?" I insist. "More messages?"

"You mean traps?" Camreon makes a face. "I don't want to find out."

"If I could get hold of one of his revenants, I could ask it where he's hiding!"

"Even if you could find him, how do you plan to kill him?" Akra adds. "He survived a fall from midair. I don't think a bullet will do the trick."

Frustrated, I pinch the bridge of my nose and squeeze my eyes shut, but when I do, I see the monk's smile as he falls: down, down, down. Shaking it off, I turn back to my brother. "I don't know how he did it," I say. "But we'll never find out if we don't go after him."

"We will," Camreon says, and my heart leaps—too soon. "But not yet."

"When?"

"When you're in better shape to face him," he replies, and the answer takes me aback.

"I told you, I'm fine—"

"No, you aren't," Camreon says, and his tone has that particular crispness it always has when he is dealing with something unpleasant. "You're combative. Impulsive. Distracted. Obsessed. You're in the grip of your malheur, and it's not safe to—"

"What do you know about my malheur?" I roar, and in the sudden silence, I feel everyone staring. Suddenly I see myself through his eyes: shouting, furious, impatient, with the blood only just washed from my hair. Shame dims the fire of my anger, and I stalk toward the hatch. "I need some air."

"Jetta . . . ," Leo calls after me, but I do not wait.

"And some space!"

As I hurry down the ladder, their voices drift after me. "I've been telling you we need to go to the lytheum mine," Theodora says.

"It's in Le Trépas's territory," Camreon replies. "And we're shorthanded as it is—"

I almost shout back up to them that I don't need the elixir, but even I know that's a lie. I'm only tired of having to rely on it. Better to learn to live without it than to live in fear of running out.

I've done it before, haven't I? In fact, I survived without the elixir for most of my life. I close my eyes and take a slow breath, then let it out, trying to focus only on the air moving through me. It's a simple tactic, but one that served me well preparing for performances. But in the dark, the monk's smile looms. My eyes snap open again, and I let out the air in a frustrated sigh.

Night has fallen while we laid our plans. The village unfolds before me in swathes of light and shadow: the silhouettes of stilted huts and grass thatch, the steeply pitched rice barns with their upswept eaves. The coronation feast is set up in the central square, on a little hillock where the rainy-season water won't pool. Paper lanterns are strung on bamboo poles, and cookfires flare under steaming pots of rice and meat and curry. Smoke and music drift on the wind. The drizzle has stopped, but the evening air is damp and cool, and my hair is still wet.

Ignoring the chill, I start toward the square, suddenly eager to join the crowd. Even when I was a small girl, I loved the closeness of strangers, especially after a show. Maman was always tired by curtain call, but Papa and I were eager to set aside our fantouches and join the audience. To hear their praise, join their chatter, share their excitement. After being in the spotlight, I could lose myself in something even greater—something outside my own mind.

But as I try to join them, the villagers part around me. I feel their eyes on the back of my head, like centipedes crawling through my hair. Of course. I am no longer a shadow player, but a nécromancien.

But as the crowd parts, I see a familiar smile at last: Tia, standing behind a table that holds a small supply of imported champagne.

The erstwhile singer is pouring glasses for the assembled crowd; she and Cheeky had insisted on hauling the last of the Boy King's bottles all the way to Malao, and now I'm glad they did. I'm equally glad that Tia is alone; I'm not quite ready to face Cheeky again.

When Tia sees me approaching, she passes me a glass, lifting her own in an Aquitan toast. "Santé!"

"À la vôtre." I'd learned the reply long ago, at Madame Audrinne's table. Lifting the glass, I take a sip. Champagne sparkles in the cup and fizzes in my nose. Before I know it, I've drained the glass.

"Champagne is meant to be savored." Tia gives me a

look that isn't quite reproach, but is far from approval. "I'm no politician, but I doubt the import rates will be favorable for a while."

"Then I should enjoy it while it lasts," I say, holding out the glass for a refill. Tia is raising the bottle when Leo's voice floats over the revelry.

"Jetta?"

Suddenly I see my thirst for what it was: another symptom. It wouldn't be the first time I'd sought calm in a bottle. "Excuse me," I say to Tia, leaving the glass on her table as I push through the crowd. But I can't outrun the feeling that Camreon was right: my malheur has crept back after all.

"Jetta?" Leo catches up with me near the cookfires. I turn reluctantly, hoping the flames hide the color of my cheeks. When he sees the look in my eyes, he reaches out to cup my face, then hesitates with his hand an inch away. A smile plays on his lips. "How much space did you need?"

With a sigh, I lean into his hand. He wraps his other arm around my shoulders, then steps back, surprised. "Your hair is still wet," he says, shrugging off his jacket.

"You don't have to take care of me, Leo."

"Let me do it anyway," he says, draping the jacket over my shoulders. It is warm, and smells like rosin and varnish.

"At least until you're ready to do it yourself."

I try to smile. "That might be awhile, considering the elixir is out of reach."

Leo raises an eyebrow. "Is it?"

"You heard Camreon," I say. "We don't have enough time or people to send them for the lytheum."

"I don't know about you, but I don't have any plans tomorrow morning." The corner of his mouth twitches upward, and my own eyes widen.

"You think we should go by ourselves?" I look back at the hut, silhouetted against the night sky, then out over the paddies and at the dark jungle beyond. "Camreon would be furious."

"When has that stopped you?" Leo says, and I can't help but laugh. "And it shouldn't change his plans. If we take the avion, we can catch up with them in Nokhor Khat by tomorrow night."

"It's too dangerous," I say, but the words are odd in my mouth—echoes of someone else's reasoning. "Isn't it?"

"Your malheur is dangerous." Coming from anyone else, his frank assessment would offend me, but Leo learned the danger in madness long before he and I met. His own maman had a similar malheur, and it led to her death. He gives me a crooked smile. "If you're going to take risks anyway, let's make them worthwhile. Meet me at the avion at dawn?"

"Why wait?" I counter, my heart beating faster as I start toward the edge of the village, where the avion is kept. But Leo catches my hand in his.

"Slow down," he says, laughing. "It's been a long day, and the docteur said you should rest, remember?"

"Right," I say, disappointed. "Dawn, then."

"I'll go stow some supplies in the avion," he says, kissing me gently before he goes. I watch him wind through the crowd, but the fire is back in my belly—from the kiss, or the champagne? Or perhaps it is only the promise of finally being able to make my own plans.

In the three weeks since my last dose of elixir, the warnings had echoed in the back of my head, and in the voices of my friends: be careful of your malheur. But perhaps I had been too careful—after all, it wasn't as if I could avoid it. The only way to tame my madness is to treat it. Wasn't it riskier, on balance, to do nothing?

The thought is freeing . . . thrilling. In fact, perhaps I have paid Camreon too much mind. He may be a king, but this is the rebellion, not the armée. I don't have to follow every order.

Especially not when I know better.

He wants to stop the deportation and take the throne, but the *Prix de Guerre* is only part of the show. It is Le Trépas pulling all the strings. And Le Trépas was last seen at the plantations.

I gaze up at the moon. The night is young; there are hours before dawn. And while Nokhor Khat is half a day away by air, the plantations are much closer. With any luck, I could be back before the champagne runs out.

Galvanized, I set off into the night—this time, away from the party. Passing through the village, I come to the paddies. The souls of frogs leap into the water as I cross the berms. In the shadows, it is hard to tell exactly where Fontaine died; the shadows hide the gore, and the mud has flowed back over the scar of the blast. But I can still smell it—the gunpowder. The blood.

"Come," I whisper, and out of the dark water, the bony head of my dragon rises.

I keep an eye on the distant village, but no one notices us out in the field. I climb up on her back, wrapping my hands around the bones of her neck as we slip away into the night.

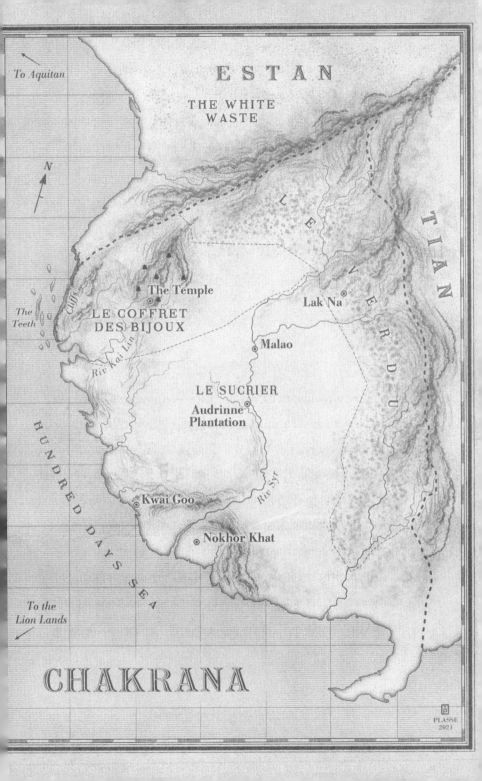

CHAPTER THREE

Applause will always be my favorite feeling, but these days, flying is a close second. It isn't just the wind in my hair or the thrill of speed, but the way Chakrana unrolls below me. The velvet jungle, the silver thread of the river, the souls glittering across all of it—the fabric of the landscape is a sequined gown on the lush body of my country. I wish others could see her as I do now.

But amid the gleam of soullight, I keep an eye out for a lightless void, for a patch of darkness. For Le Trépas. I can't shake the thought I'll catch sight of him with every passing bend in the river.

Traveling south, the jungle gives way to plantation estates as we pass into Le Sucrier—the rich fields around the Riv Syr that the Aquitans claimed for sugar. From the air, I can still see the outlines of the berms that used to divide the fields into paddies when rice was planted here. Now, cane stands like soldiers, stiff and stately and tall enough to harvest.

The Audrinnes' house is easy to spot from a distance. Outside the famed architecture of Nokhor Khat or the woven banyan temple of the Maiden, it's the grandest building I've seen. The pale structure sits at the end of a long drive flanked by mimosa trees, lined with columns and archways over a wide veranda and fronted with a curved cul-de-sac. On the nights the Audrinnes hosted our shadow plays, fine families from nearby estates would pull up in stately carriages, spilling out onto the steps, and the air would buzz with laughter and anticipation.

Of course, I was more familiar with the servants' entrance at the back. We would make our way through the bustle of the kitchens, carrying our fantouches and our instruments unseen to the stage in the great room. Now the house is quiet, the only movement the wind in the grass and the souls drifting by. I am so used to their light that it takes me a moment to realize the lamps in the great room are burning.

Instantly I crouch over the dragon's neck, as though to hide. Foolish—as if anyone watching wouldn't notice the dragon herself, silhouetted against the moon. But as we pass over the house, nothing stirs except the dead.

Then who lit the lamps? Could the Audrinnes have been spared? Somehow I doubt it. Their estate is by far the largest in the area, and very hard to miss. I circle one more time, trying to get a better view—or to see if there are corpses in the fields. But the sugar could easily hide a body, even if it was standing upright.

I am banking for another pass when I see the horses. They stand on the wide drive: two matched mares, pale as cream. Monsieur Audrinne had them shipped all the way from Aquitan to pull his wife's carriage. Now they wander free to roam—or to be eaten by an enterprising tiger. There is no way Madame would let them loose. Not if she was still alive.

The horses flee as we drop lower, their white tails streaming like flags of surrender. The servants' entry is closest, but I steer my dragon toward the curved driveway at the front of the house.

In a clatter of bones, the creature lands, long claws gouging clods from the packed dirt. I throw my leg over her ridged back and slide to the ground. My dragon sniffs the air—or pretends to. After all, there is no flesh on her hollow skull, no lungs in the sinuous cage of her ribs. But her soul contains her memory, her habits . . . her instinct. As she lowers her head, she shifts on her claws, uneasy. I scan the estate, but there is no movement aside from the wind in the leaves and the clouds gliding across the stars. "Shh," I murmur to the dragon. "Stay."

At my command, she hunkers down as though to hide, this great beast with bones that gleam in the silver starlight. Perhaps I shouldn't be surprised she is nervous, out here in the open. But as far as I can see, we are alone except for the souls and the horses.

I start toward the wide stairs. There used to be a Chakran porter stationed at the heavy mahogany doors, to welcome Madame's guests to the show. Tonight the doors are shut tight, and the polished wood is marred by paint. No . . . blood. It drips, thick and clotted, across the paneled wood, in a now-familiar symbol: know your enemy.

Le Trépas has been here—is he here still? I try the handle, but the door is locked. I'll be taking the servants' entrance after all. Back down the stairs, I turn toward the north side of the house. My feet sink into the green grass of the soft lawn as I pass by the arched openings of the veranda. I falter when I reach the windows of the great room. The gas lamps are now off.

My scalp prickles; I whirl, but there is no one behind me. My dragon waits for me on the drive—the horses have stopped, nervous, under the mimosa trees. And souls are still drifting by. Le Trépas is nowhere near. But the armée had said they'd seen other corpses. . . .

If I can catch one and pull out the soul, it might be able to tell me where the old monk is. And if I find Le Trépas, the war is over, and so are my nightmares. I will finally be able to close my eyes without his knowing smile lurking in the darkness there.

I creep closer to the rail of the veranda, but when I reach the windows, I'm not tall enough to see over the sill. Then a breeze stirs my hair, rippling through the night-blooming jasmine that cascades down the side of the house. Under the perfume of the flowers wafts a sweeter smell: the scent of rot. And still I feel eyes on the back of my head. Yet there is nothing on the lawn, and no one. Only the path, and the mimosa trees, and the carriage house off to the side . . . but its doors are shut. How did Madame's horses escape?

My mouth is dry; I wet my lips, wishing briefly for the glass of champagne I left on the table. Then I set out toward the carriage house, souls drifting in my wake.

The squat building is made of brick and set with wide wooden doors; only Aquitans would build with brick in Chakrana. I look for a crack around the hinges or in the shuttered windows—some way to peer inside—but the building is well kept. Still, the smell wafts out, stronger now. Death.

I grab the handle, then think better of it—I've learned my lesson about rushing in. Drawing my little knife, I make a shallow cut in line with the older scars on my left hand. Air hisses through my teeth as blood wells up, black in the moonlight, like spilled ink on the pale palette of my palm. Tucking my knife back into my belt, I dip a finger in the blood and mark the door with the symbol of life. Eagerly, the soul of a barn rat scuttles in. I step back into the shadows and whisper to it, "Open."

The door swings wide, but nothing springs out. Creeping closer, I peer inside. Thin moonlight barely pushes through the shutters, but the souls of mice glimmer in the grain bin, and the spirits of flies zip through the air alongside the living ones. The dim glow illuminates a figure standing in one of the horse stalls, and the straw is not as golden as her hair.

Madame Audrinne was always lovely in the way the Aquitans prize: plump and pale and proud, with those wide foreign eyes. Cornflower blue, she used to say, though we don't have cornflowers in Chakrana. My old patroness is still pale, still plump. But her eyes are a different blue—like cold fire.

The look in them chills me, but underneath the fear is something even colder: grief. She didn't deserve this sort of death—no one does. Still, I dare not let down my guard. Though her face is familiar, the soul behind it is a mystery.

Whoever—whatever—it is, I could free it if I can get close enough. Cautiously, I approach, blood still wet on my finger. She reaches out over the stall door, but her own hands have been cut from her wrists; she cannot lift the latch to escape. All the better. But is this another trap Le Trépas has laid? Her mouth opens as she takes a labored breath, and I am relieved to see nothing behind her teeth but her blackened tongue.

"Jetta," she whispers through cracked lips. "Jetta of the Ros Nai."

At the name of my troupe, I freeze. "Madame?" My own reply is a croak. "Madame Audrinne?"

"Oui, ma cher," she says in Aquitan, with the same gracious affection she always displayed. "It's so good to see you after so long. Are you still performing? When this unpleasantness is past, we must have another show. For now, be a dear and open the door."

I blink, gathering my thoughts as she scrabbles fruitlessly at the latch. It must be Madame's spirit in her own corpse—I can't imagine anyone else imitating her style. But her ice-blue eyes give away the vengeful nature of her soul. Her death had not been easy.

My stomach clenches at the thought. She had always been kind to me, and generous with payment—this Aquitan beauty, rich with Chakran wealth. The Audrinnes represented everything the rebellion was fighting against, but this was not the way to win the war. "What happened to you?"

Madame's laugh is still musical, though the notes are duller in a dead throat. "The soldiers locked me in here," she says. "Can you imagine?"

I take a shallow breath—the smell of death is so strong. "I meant . . . with Le Trépas."

"Le Trépas?" The word is a snake's hiss, and her lip curls at the mention of the monk. "He made me a lesson to my fool of a husband, who ran off to fight the deportation in Nokhor Khat. Let me out," she adds then, still dragging the stump of her wrist across the latch. "I can still take revenge on the man who made me a target, even if I cannot kill the one who held the knife."

"You want to kill your husband?" Is she telling the truth, or is it only some ploy Le Trépas has dreamed up? "Why not the nécromancien?"

"He's immortal," she says, with a regretful smile. "Open the door."

"Immortal?" I stare at her, my mind racing. Le Trépas had claimed to be a god, to be able to cheat death—but I had thought those were the ravings of a man hungry for power. Then again, my own blood has given Akra similar protection. Had Le Trépas somehow used the last drops of my blood on his own skin? "How can you be sure?"

"Rumors have flown in recent weeks from soldiers moving south. Not the Aquitan ones," she says quickly. "But the Chakrans. You know how they are, with their superstitions. . . ." She trails off, her wrist going still against the latch. Then she laughs again, softly now.

"I suppose I should have listened after all. But my husband said it was only a charlatan's trick, and so I believed him. That is, until I stabbed the man through the heart. The nécromancien," she adds, resuming her work on the latch. "Not my husband. Let me go so I can correct the mistake."

The image sets me back on my heels: Madame Audrinne with blood on her hands, Le Trépas pulling the blade from his scarred chest. If he has used my blood to bind his soul to his skin, my blood will bring it back out. Just as it will free Madame Audrinne.

"I'll let you go," I tell her truthfully. "Just tell me where he is, first."

"South," she says, raising one missing hand to her dead heart. "His presence pulls at me. Open the door and I'll lead you there."

South. Likely in the capital, as Camreon had guessed. But at least we had confirmation now. I reach out, and the corpse smiles, but I take hold of her blackened wrist and not the latch. As her brow furrows, I use my bloody finger to trace the mark: the circle of death.

The symbol still makes me uneasy—after all, it is one Le Trépas had taught me. But as Madame's body falls into the straw, I do not imagine the look of relief on her face. Freed, her soul is a gold light, illuminating the carriage house. Madame had come from Lephare; she had always loved the lights.

Only now do I unlatch the door, letting her soul drift free. I am about to leave the carriage house myself when a voice crashes through the dark. "Put your hands over your head!"

Startled, I whirl, falling back against the stall door; it swings wide, banging against the wall as I land hard on my tailbone. Half a second later, another bang, and a flash of light. Grit stings my cheek as a bullet buries itself in the brick beside me.

"Over your head!"

This time I obey the man standing in the doorway. My heart pounds as I piece him together: the armée uniform, the black leather boots, the smoke still rising from the pistol in his hand. But above the olive-green jacket, a Chakran face. Relief floods in. "You scared me, brother."

"I'm not your brother," the soldier spits, jerking his chin at Madame's body. In his hand, the gun trembles. "I saw what you did. I know who you are!"

No use denying it, then. "I won't hurt you," I say, keeping my voice calm. Steady. "I'm nothing like Le Trépas."

The soldier tenses at the mention of the old monk. "Do you have any weapons?"

"A knife in my belt," I say, hoping he doesn't notice the blood on my fingers. The souls of flies buzz by Madame's corpse; if I can draw one into the blade, I can order it to cut the soldier's throat. "Do you want me to toss it to you?"

"Don't move," he says quickly. Had I been too eager? The soldier wets his lips. "Are you alone?"

"Of course not," I say with a scoff. It's a lie, but I'm a good actor. I glance over his shoulder through the open door, an expectant look on my face. "The others are searching the grounds, but they must have heard the shot. They'll be here any moment."

The soldier shifts on his feet, nervous. What does he imagine creeping up behind him? Rebels—or revenants? Still, he keeps his eyes locked on mine. "Come closer."

"The rebellion offers clemency to anyone who joins—"

"Closer!" he shouts. "And keep your hands up."

"All right," I say quickly. The soldier watches every movement as I rise to my feet, hands still over my head. Reluctantly, I slide my feet through the straw, hoping he will lower his weapon before he tries to take my knife. But he keeps his gun trained on me as he paws at the blade in my belt.

Even without the knife, there is still a drop of blood on the tip of my finger. Could I pull his living soul right from his skin? I have never tried it. It should be no different than killing the soldier with a knife, and the gods know I've killed before. But Le Trépas is the one who kills with his blood, and I am nothing like him. Nothing. As I hesitate, I hear feet approaching outside. More soldiers—but I smile anyway. "That's the other rebels now."

At last the soldier turns to check. I grab for the gun. Wrong move—he's stronger than I am. As we wrestle for the weapon, he fires wildly. The bullet disappears into the rafters.

Then he punches me in the ribs.

Gasping, I stumble back, startled to see my knife in the soldier's fist. Is that blood on the blade? I press a shaking hand to my side. It comes away warm and wet. But when I meet the soldier's eyes; he looks as surprised as I am. "Let the gods forgive me," he murmurs, like a prayer.

Then the soldiers outside call his name. "Sunan?"

"Aides-moi!" he shouts back. "It's the nécromancien!"

Pale faces appear at the edges of the doorway, both Aquitan. They'd sent the Chakran in first, and it's good for me that they did. The Aquitans never cared about our gods. They wouldn't have hesitated to shoot.

They don't hesitate now—not even with Sunan in the line of fire.

As they lift their guns, I lunge for the cover of the stall. The Chakran soldier is not so quick. I hear the bullets thudding into his flesh; he is dead before he hits the ground. His soul stands over his body, as though surprised, but I don't have time for shock. My hand darts out to draw the symbol of life on the young man's skin. Air gurgles in his throat as his soul pours back into his flesh.

He arches his back, opening his mouth. Blood is all that comes out. Still, his voice echoes in my head, like Akra's voice does—part of our new connection. "Let me go," he whispers in my skull; the same plea Madame had made. But I am not so lenient with Sunan.

"I'll let you go when the others are dead," I gasp, short of breath. The wound in my side is starting to throb.

Groaning, Sunan lifts the gun, rising to his feet like a broken marionette. His body jerks and judders as the soldiers fire, but this time he shoots back. The Aquitans cry out as they fall, one, then the other, but the Chakran only stops firing when he runs out of bullets.

My ears ring in the sudden silence. Sunan sags against the wall, his shoulders heaving. Blood covers his chest and runs down his face from the empty socket of his eye. With the uniform, with the haircut, with the shadows of the carriage house, I see my brother instead—the way he looked when he died, and when I'd brought him back.

Remorse stabs through me, sharper than the knife. I have held so tightly to the differences between myself and Le Trépas—the way he makes the dead walk, while I make them live again. But life isn't always such a gift.

More gunfire rings out, closer to the veranda this time. The Chakran soldier stumbles to the doorway, pulling one of the rifles from the fallen men. Sliding down along the doorframe, he fires. As the gun cracks, cries drift in from outside. But Sunan's finger is slipping on the trigger, wet with blood; his arm shakes, unable to hold steady. How much longer can he fight? How many soldiers are left?

Then, even louder than the gunfire—the blast of a grenade. My heart clenches in fear, but the carriage house is unaffected . . . at least, so far. Gritting my teeth, I prop myself on one hand. Blood has already soaked through the fabric of my sarong. Crawling to the window, I pull myself up with the sill, easing open the shutter. There is a bright light among the mimosa trees. Not an explosion or a fire, but the soul of my dragon.

"No!" The soldiers must have found her—why had I ordered her to stay? Her spirit makes shadows of the figures like dark wraiths under the trees. Then a pale hand rips the shutter back, revealing another soldier pressed up against the brick exterior of the carriage house. He swears, raising his pistol just as another shot rings out. The soldier crumples to the ground.

I duck back beneath the windowsill, breathing hard, with Sunan's voice echoing in my head. "Release me."

"There are still soldiers out there," I pant.

"They're dead," he insists. "Let me go."

I glance to the window, but looking out seems unwise. Instead, I creep back through the straw toward the doorway where Sunan's body sits. Peering over his shoulder, I look for movement, seeing nothing.

"I can't lie to you," he says, and there is a hitch in his voice. "Please."

I hesitate, but I don't want to be a liar either. So I take his hand in mine, and his skin is so slick with blood that the mark of death shows pale in a sea of red. The body sighs as the soul rises. After that, silence. I press my hand to my side and wait.

Why were the soldiers here in the first place? Were they

part of Fontaine's battalion, or working with Le Trépas? I should have asked before Sunan's soul fled. Still, other spirits cluster, closing in. Flies and mice, birds and a prowling cat. The dragon's soul stalks brightly across the lawn. Can I draw her back into the blackened bones? I have to, if I'm going to meet Leo at the avion.

I should treat my wound—do something to staunch the blood. Wet warmth trickles down my side. How long until sunrise? I glance to the sky, but I can't remember which way is east. Thoughts are hard to string together. A breeze through the door moves the haze of gun smoke like a curtain, bringing the incongruous smell of jasmine . . . and Leo's voice.

"Jetta?" For a moment, I'm sure I'm imagining it. Then I hear him cursing in Chakran and Aquitan. "She's in the carriage house!"

Frowning, I squint through the soullight and the smoke to see him pelting across the lawn. I scoff a little, incredulous, but the movement hurts. "How many times do I have to tell you?" I say as my eyes slide shut. "It's not your job to take care of me."

INCIDENT REPORT REGARDING TEMPLE FOURTEEN
Capitaine Bertrand Audrinne

My men and I arrived yesterday afternoon at our first assigned location: Temple Fourteen, half a kilometer northwest of Nokhor Khat, and dedicated to the deity known as the Keeper of Knowledge. In order to free the locals from the grip of their superstitions, our orders were to destroy any false idols, dismantle the altar, and arrest any monks in the area. However, upon initial inspection, our work seemed to have been done for us.

Further search this morning in the surrounding villages led us to a single monk, identified by the traditional tattoos on his back. We have taken him into custody, and he insists he is the only one left in the area. According to him, the others were killed years ago, not by the armée, but by Le Trépas himself.

Additionally, he claims the man desecrated

the temple by opening the altar and stealing their religious book, supposedly bound in the skin of the very deity to which the temple has been dedicated: a Book of Knowledge, if you will. He says that this book is how Le Trépas gained so much power. Unfortunately, the monk died before the questioneur could glean any more information about the book's contents.

With Le Trépas himself in custody, it might be worth questioning him as to the current location of this artifact. It's clearly an important symbol to the religious fringe; indeed, the monk we captured seems to believe that the soul of the Keeper of Knowledge can be found inside the book.

As to our orders, my men and I will be finished at Temple Fourteen much sooner than anticipated. Our next assignment is Temple Thirty-Four, to the northeast. You can expect my next report upon our arrival there.

CHAPTER FOUR

The soft sound of a violin—a distantly familiar tune—makes me open my eyes. When I do, I am gazing at Aquitan.

A painting of Lephare, to be exact. City of Lights. The artist has captured it at dawn, gilding each gabled roof and the tall spire of their famous cathedral. I know the work well—it hangs over Madame Audrinne's velvet settee.

I am lying on the couch in the great room. Morning light gleams through the expensive glass of the tall windows. The wooden floors glow honey gold under the scattered armée bedrolls. The soldiers must have been camping out here.

Had they thought that the last time they'd see Lephare was in the gilded frame?

Once I had hoped to travel there myself. Now the dream of visiting Aquitan is at least as distant as my life as a shadow player. Still, this room was where that dream began, inspired by another work of art on the walls: a depiction of Les Chanceux, the spring that treats madness. Theodora's uncle—Le Roi Fou, the mad King of Aquitan—takes the waters there. When Madame Audrinne had first told me the story, I had assumed it was magic that kept Le Roi's madness at bay, and not the lytheum salts dissolved in the water.

Madame Audrinne . . . the memories of last night surface slowly, like bodies in a still pond. The soldier, the fight . . . my hand goes to my ribs; the makeshift bandage there has a floral pattern that matches the curtains on the high windows. Gingerly, I prod at the dressing to try to gauge the severity of the knife wound underneath. The pain makes me gasp.

"Just rest," Leo says gruffly, his face looming into my vision. He holds the neck of a violin in his hand, and now I recognize the music I'd heard earlier: the broken melody of the song he'd been working on the last few weeks, so new it doesn't even have a name. "The Audrinnes had some excellent medical supplies, but you've lost a lot of blood."

"I didn't lose it," I reply with a twist of a smile. "It's in the carriage house."

Leo doesn't laugh at my joke. "You could have died out there."

"Could have, would have . . ." The look on his face stops me short. "I didn't, though."

"Because Cam and I found you first!"

My heart sinks. I can already imagine Camreon's disappointment. "Where is he?"

"Trying to string the dragon back together," Leo says, and I wince at the memory of the blast. Leo kneels beside the couch so that we're eye to eye. "What were you thinking, running off alone?"

"It was your idea in the first place!"

"It was?" Theodora's voice surprises me; I hadn't realized she was here too. I lift my head from the arm of the settee to find her seated at the writing desk, flipping delicately through a stack of old papers with ink-stained fingers. The painting of Les Chanceux hangs just above her, but it looks strange to me. Smaller than I remember. "You didn't mention that part, Leonin."

"I wanted to take her to the lytheum mine," he replies stiffly. "Perhaps you can see why."

"I had to know what happened here," I say, defensive.

"Was it worth the risk?"

"There were clues, just like I thought." The memories are coming in a wave. I push upright again—my ribs throb, but I ignore the pain. "Madame told me the monk is immortal."

"Immortal?" I can hear the curiosity in Theodora's voice. "That *is* interesting."

Leo turns to his sister. "Do you mind?"

"Well, it is," Theodora says mildly, still looking down at the papers on the desk. "And if it's true, we'll have to come up with a long-term solution to keep him locked away safely. I wonder if he found the secret of immortality in the book."

"What book?" I ask. Leo throws his hands in the air, sitting down hard on a nearby ottoman, his back to both of us. Theodora ignores him, turning to me.

"I've been looking through Monsieur Audrinne's paperwork. He served in the armée under my father. . . ." Her voice breaks on the word. General Legarde—the elder General Legarde, her father and Leo's—had died only a few months before their brother.

In the silence, Leo returns to his violin, plucking out a few gentle notes, and his sister swallows, gathering herself to continue.

"Some of Audrinne's incident reports are from just after La Victoire," she says. "Apparently Le Trépas stole a book from the Keeper of Knowledge."

"Where is it now?" I ask her, but she shrugs.

"I haven't found anything else that mentions it. Still, wouldn't a Book of Knowledge be fascinating?" A familiar sparkle lights her eyes—one that had been missing in the last few weeks. She turns to me. "Do you remember seeing my father's old journals? He wrote about overseeing the destruction of the temples after La Victoire. I often got the sense that he was searching for something. I wonder if it was the book."

"We can assume he never found it," Leo interjects, his head still bent over the violin. "Or they'd both still be here."

Even without saying their names, I know Leo means his brother and father. So does Theodora. "You don't have to sound so pleased," she says through her teeth.

"I'm not." The strings are louder than his voice, as though the instrument can speak for him. The notes of an Aquitan hymn . . . the song he'd played the night he shot Xavier. "But there was no other way to stop them."

"Of course you tell yourself that," Theodora replies stiffly. "Otherwise the guilt would eat you alive."

"Guilty? Me? No," Leo says with a bitter twist of his lips. "*I've* never killed an innocent man."

Theodora's face goes pale, but before she can object, Camreon clears his throat. He stands in the hall just outside the greatroom, as though the tension between Le Fleur and her brother was thick enough to bar the way. But Theodora turns back to the papers on the desk, her cheeks bright pink, while Leo keeps plucking the strings. As Camreon steps into the room on silent feet, he turns to me. "You're awake."

"I'm not, actually," I reply, bracing myself for a lecture. "I'm just a very good actor."

"A terrible rebel, though." To my surprise, a smile quirks his lips. "Luckily, it looks like all our casualties will survive."

"The dragon?" I say quickly, and he nods.

"Dragon bone is remarkably strong," he says mildly. Automatically, I glance to his brow, where the crown had rested, but he has laid it aside for now. While the coronation clearly needed a king, a rescue mission was best suited to the Tiger. "The skeleton is a little singed, but still sound."

The relief that washes over me is more powerful than I'd expected—I'd grown rather fond of the dragon in the last few weeks. "Do you need me to ensoul her again?" I ask, but Camreon shakes his head.

"It's already taken care of."

"You used my blood?"

"You left plenty of it lying around," he says, pulling something long and slim out of his pocket. "Besides, I didn't want the dragon's soul straying too far. I didn't know how long you'd be asleep."

My brow furrows. "Is that a fountain pen?"

"Not my finest inventions," Theodora says critically, holding out a second pen with a flourish: a slender bit of brass, with a nib on one end and a point on the other. Craning my neck, I can see the inkwell among the papers on the desk, and the blotter stained in black and muddy red. "But they might be my most powerful. There's enough blood in both of them for two or three fantouches."

My hand goes to the tiny scar in the crook of my arm, where an armée docteur let my blood into a jar. A queasy feeling spreads in my stomach. But this is not the armée— these are my friends. "It should come in handy," I say at last.

"It should," Cam agrees, tucking his own pen back into his pocket. "Considering we won't have you with us."

I stiffen. "What?"

"Leo and I will be taking the dragon back to Malao to gather the others for our trip to the capital. You and

Theodora will take the avion to the lytheum mine." Camreon gives me a wry look, but I turn instead to the painting of Les Chanceux. The languid women stare back, uncaring. My mind reels. How can my friends go without me? They need me—and I need them.

"Leo," I say. He has always been my staunchest ally. "I thought you promised to look out for me."

To my great annoyance, he grins. "And you promised to meet me at the avion, but here we are."

"Leo!"

"Jetta." Putting his violin back in the case, he comes to my side, pushing my hair back from my forehead. His hands are so cool on my skin. "It may not feel like it, but I *am* looking out for you. You need your elixir, and you're safer out of the fight. Besides, this way your song will be a surprise."

My brow furrows. "My song?"

"You've heard me working on it, haven't you?" He nods toward his violin, and I can almost hear the notes echoing in my head, the gentle falling melody he's been picking out. Then he squeezes my fingers. "So far I've had my hands a little too full to finish."

I raise a skeptical eyebrow. "You think you'll have time

between freeing the Aquitans and helping Cam seize the throne?"

"I'll make time, I promise. The next time you see me, it will be finished," he says. "*If* you promise to find your elixir."

I chew my lip, but I don't have much choice. "I promise," I say at last, and he smiles.

"Bien." He squeezes my hand once more, then stands. "Akra will be coming with us, so we can keep in touch through him."

"Have him check in regularly, Leonin," Theodora says. "You know that Jetta can't call to him unless he's listening. And if you find Xavier . . ." As she trails off, Leo braces himself, but after a moment, she holds out the second pen. "You know what to do."

With his free hand, he takes the pen, emotions flickering across his face. "Theod—"

"Take care of yourself, Leonin," she says, turning abruptly toward the door. "Come, Cam. I'll walk you to the avion. While you were working on the dragon, I was reading Audrinne's old reports. . . ."

As they disappear down the hall, Leo watches after his sister, trouble brewing in his dark eyes. It pulls at my heart— he'd had to kill his brother to save his people. It wasn't fair he might lose his sister too. "Are you all right, Leo?"

My question seems to startle him. He looks down at me, trying to smile, but I can see the pain behind it. "You don't have to take care of me, Jetta," he teases, and I can't help but laugh.

"Do I at least get a goodbye kiss?" I ask him, and his smile turns real.

"Never goodbye," he says, leaning down to grant my request. The kiss is soft—almost careful. But then he buries his face in my hair, pressing his heart to mine as he holds me tight. His whisper is a breath in my ear. "Only au revoir."

"Until we meet again." Remembering his old promise, I wrap my own arms around him, more tightly than I ought to, but it's easy to ignore the pain in my ribs for the pounding of my heart. We are interrupted by the sound of Theodora clearing her throat, and for a moment I wonder if I can let Leo go.

But his sister taps her foot in the doorway, arms crossed. "Ready?"

"No," Leo says lightly, and when he pulls away, it feels like my heart is going with him. Are those tears in his eyes? He dashes them away with his free hand, still smiling. "But it's time to go anyway."

As he slips his fingers from my grasp, I open my hand to let him. He grabs his violin case, lifting it in a salute, and disappears down the hall.

With a sigh, I sit back against the velvet arm of the settee. Then I catch sight of Theodora. When she sees me looking, she turns away quickly, but I've already seen the tears in her eyes. "You can likely still catch him, if you have more to say."

"Nothing I say can make my brother less a monster," she says stiffly, and suddenly every muscle in my body is tense.

"Leo is not a monster." My voice is a low growl, but Theodora only shakes her head.

"I wasn't talking about Leo."

As Theodora wipes her eyes with her wrist, I look at her anew. She hasn't been herself the last few weeks; then again, neither have I. But I know why she is coming with me to the mine, rather than going to Nokhor Khat with the others. Hard enough for her when Xavier died the first time.

"Do you want to talk about it?" I say at last, but the girl only grimaces, gesturing to the floral-patterned dressing on my ribs.

"You're bleeding again. Let me change your bandage and get you more painkiller."

I sit back in silence. As she ministers to my wound, I stare at the painting of Les Chanceux—the lovely women, the sapphire pool—and I know what it's like to mourn something you never really had to begin with.

Dear Maman and Papa,

It is strange, in a way, to join the rebellion only to resurrect a tradition I started while in the armée. But writing to you before a mission has always been a comfort, and while most of my letters never found their way home, I did, eventually. So I thought I would continue the tradition. Just in case.

    We're traveling to Nokhor Khat tonight to stop the deportation of the Aquitans. That's a sentence I never thought I'd write, but Camreon hopes that the Aquitans will join us if we pull them out of the fire. With Le Trépas on the loose, quite a few of the rebels have disappeared back into the jungle. I can't blame them for being afraid—for trying to protect their families. I would do anything to protect ours. But with no armée at his back, Camreon is a paper tiger.

    Jetta will not be coming with us. Before you worry, she is well enough. Before you call me a liar, she has been better. Cheeky actually suggested sending her home so you could keep an eye on her, but I don't dare mention the idea to Jetta. After all, she's practically the only thing that can kill me.

This way, at least, she's out of the fray. Theodora is taking her to find her elixir. Don't worry—I will keep in touch with her our usual way. I'm also going to send Miu to you. You remember the fantouche Jetta ensouled? There is no way to bring her with us, and you could use the company. And this way, if you don't hear from us for a little while, you can watch the fantouche, and know that Jetta's still alive as well.

As for me, you'll just have to keep your fingers crossed.

I'm joking. I'll be fine, and with any luck, this will all be over soon. The next time I write, it will likely be with an invitation to toast the new king in Nokhor Khat, and tickets to a show at the Royal Opera. Then we can all take turns watching out for Jetta. Until then, she and I will look out for each other.

Your son,

Akra

ACT 1,
SCENE 5

The rebels have spent most of the night on dragonback to travel from Malao to Nokhor Khat. Now the moon is setting, and the rainy-season drizzle masks the fading stars. The dragon slips easily through the tattered clouds. Though her once-white bones are singed and blackened, and the tip of her long tail is missing, her soul is as strong as ever.

From his vantage point astride her neck, CAMREON steers her in a wide circle around the capital. LEO keeps glancing back north, while AKRA grimly refuses to look down. CHEEKY and TIA peer eagerly at the city as their silk sarongs ripple in the wind.

Nokhor Khat sits in the broken bowl of an old caldera. Jungle lines the northeast slopes, and the Hundred Days Sea pours into a protected bay to the south. The dark mass of the fort looms over the water, ostensibly to protect the Ruby Palace and the old temple of Hell's Court, but the Aquitan stronghold had always seemed more like a threat.

Artillerie lines the parapets, but the guns are unmanned, and the once-busy harbor now cradles a single ship: the Prix de Guerre, *which had carried weapons and warbirds from Aquitan. Now she waits, empty and quiet like most of the city.*

TIA: When I was here last, Nokhor Khat was full of light.

LEO: It's three in the morning.

TIA: Precisely when you need light most.

The showgirl shakes her head in mock disappointment. The passing breeze ruffles her short black hair; it's grown a little in the three months since she last saw the city. Back then, she'd been disguised as a boy, to conform to the Aquitan's limiting sense of decorum. Now the Aquitans are on the run, and diamonds glint in her ears.

I wonder how long it will be before the city gleams like it used to.

CHEEKY glares at her.

CHEEKY: Well, it's my first time, so let me enjoy it.

TIA *(teasing)*: I bet you say that to all the cities.

LEO grins back at them.

LEO: This is a rebel foray, not your vaudeville act!

AKRA: As long as it's not a tragedy. Where are we landing?

CAMREON: Le Livre—the inn near the dock. The proprietor is friendly to the rebellion.

TIA: And his daughter is friendly to out-of-work singers.

CHEEKY turns, wide-eyed, to stare at TIA.

CHEEKY: I knew there was a reason you insisted on coming back!

TIA: I'm a lover, not a fighter.

AKRA leans forward to point at the fort on the horizon.

AKRA: If the armée has even one lookout, you won't get a choice in the matter. The moonlight is behind us.

CAMREON: That's why we're coming by water. Lift your packs.

As the dragon approaches the harbor, CAM coaxes her down until her claws ruffle the waves. LEO raises his violin high, and CHEEKY grits her teeth in a silent shriek as the creature sinks into the water of the bay.

Half submerged, the dragon slips past the docks, the rebels clinging to her spine. They pass close to the fort, but if there are lookouts, they are watching for a ship, not a sea serpent. The crocodiles that make their home in the brackish bay scatter before the larger reptile. But when the dragon reaches the moon bridge at the top of the harbor, she stops, lifting her head from the water: a net of heavy chain sits just below the water line.

Curious, the beast presses her bony nose into the water gate, *but CAMREON stops her as the chain rattles, loud in the night.*

CAMREON: Shhh.

TIA *(whispering)*: Would Jetta's blood open the lock?

LEO: Don't waste it. The inn is close. We can walk from here.

Nudging the dragon toward the reedy bank, CAMREON climbs lightly up her neck to the muddy shore. AKRA and LEO follow, reaching back to help the girls. They wring water from the edges of their sarongs as the dragon nestles happily into the silt.

CHEEKY: I'm soaking wet.

TIA: What's new?

CAMREON: Shh!

The streets are eerily quiet, even for the late hour. No drunks stumble through the alleys, no secret trysts happen in the shadows. No one collects trash or treasure from the gutters—there aren't even any soldiers on patrol as the rebels make their way to the inn.

Le Livre is a low-slung plantation-style building, surrounded by a lush garden thick with palms and dripping with orchids. In better days, the shutters would be open, and a lamp was always lit at the door. But now the light has gone out, and the garden is overgrown. CAM ducks under the overhanging vines, pushing back the rain hood of his coat as he makes his way to the back door.

TIA: It's strange to see the lamp dark.

CAMREON: They're likely short on space with all the refugees in town, but Siris has always made room for rebels at Le Livre.

CHEEKY: We know Tia will be fine with sharing a bed.

TIA: Shh!

TIA hangs back from the door, suddenly nervous.

She'll hear you.

CHEEKY's eyes go even wider.

CHEEKY: She doesn't know?

CAMREON: Quiet, or you're both sleeping on the riverbank.

Raising his hand, CAM knocks at the door. Once, twice. He waits, frowning, then knocks again. No answer. He glances back at LEO, who shrugs one shoulder.

LEO: It's not like Siris to not have someone awake in the kitchen.

CAMREON hesitates, then raises his hand once more. Before

he can knock yet again, the door opens at last. But it is not SIRIS standing inside.

Instead, a woman frowns at him—a little older than the rebels, but quite a bit richer, judging from the fine fabric of the robe she's wearing. Her long brown hair and wide eyes give away her mixed parentage. This is ELLISIA, though CAM doesn't know it yet.

ELLISIA: If you're looking for rooms, there are none.

CHEEKY shoots TIA a mischievous glance.

CHEEKY: She's rude. I like her already.

ELLISIA overhears—as CHEEKY has meant her to. She narrows her eyes.

ELLISIA: If you're looking for work, come back tomorrow.

TIA hisses to CHEEKY.

TIA: That isn't her!

ELLISIA tries to shut the door, but CAM puts his foot between it and the jamb.

CAMREON: We're looking for Siris, actually.

ELLISIA: He isn't here. And you're getting water on his floor.

She looks pointedly at CAMREON's foot, then leans on the door, trying to close it. But LEO steps into the light spilling through the crack.

LEO: Ellisia?

She frowns, looking up in surprise.

ELLISIA: Leo? What are you doing here?

Looking back toward the street, she pulls the door open.

Come in. Quickly.

CHAPTER SIX

I wake with applause roaring in my ears, only to find my cheek pressed against the cold metal of the avion. It takes me a moment to recognize the smell in the wind on my face: the briny scent of the sea. It was not the roar of applause I'd heard, but the rolling waves of the ocean.

I take a deep breath through my nose, then put a hand over my aching ribs. The painkiller I'd taken before getting into the avion is wearing off. We had left the plantation just after sunset, heavy with provisions raided from the Audrinnes' larder. I had wanted to help Theodora pack, but she insisted that I first change out of my sarong, stiff with blood. Wrestling into a dress from Madame's closet had left me sweating, and so I had ignored Theodora's I-told-you-so look and let her load the avion herself.

She had used the opportunity to take control of the flying machine; as Camreon had said, there was plenty of blood lying around. Now Theodora guides the bird easily over the landscape. I glance past the wings, trying to get a sense of where we are . . . there, to the right. The open water of the Hundred Days Sea. The jungle tumbles green and wild in the jagged valleys just off the other side of the avion; we are skirting the shoreline west of Nokhor Khat.

Theodora sits in the front seat, glancing between the map in her hands and the land below. "Are we close?" I call over the breeze.

She looks back at me, as though surprised I am awake. "I think so, but this is our second pass. Keep an eye on the sea cliffs, will you? We're looking for a cavern near the waterline, but it's hard to find in the dark."

I peer down at the cliffs, black and dramatic above the booming waves. They are formed of old lava rock, brittle and broken. Years ago, Chakrana was forged in fire, but the jungle has covered much of the country, leaving only the old tunnels beneath the surface. They stretch for miles and miles. "How did you find the lytheum in the first place?"

"Luck and legend, put together," Theodora replies, and the gleam is back in her eye. "Which doesn't sound very scientific, unless you know anything about science. Lytheum salts are often found in ashstone and other pyroxenes. So I knew to look near volcanic activity . . . but of course in Chakrana, that's almost everywhere. You're laughing at me."

"What? No!" I try to press my lips flat, but she's caught me off guard. Or maybe it's the height making me giddy. "I just . . . haven't seen you this happy in a while. Talking about . . . pyroxenes."

She gives me a sidelong look. "I prefer them to politics."

"So do I," I insist. "Go on."

Theodora frowns, but she can't resist. "Well. By chance, I overheard a story from one of my father's lieutenants about a village nearby called Kwai Goo. The Chakran name translates to Happy Valley, and that made me start thinking. You're still laughing."

"I'm smiling," I say, and then I do laugh. "Only because you're *always* thinking. That's not a bad thing!"

"Know your enemy and know yourself, and you'll have nothing to fear," she says archly. "But if you know everything, you'll have a hundred new questions by morning. Xavier used to say that to me," she adds, more quietly now. Then she scrubs a hand down over her face. "Anyway, with some research, I found that the water source for the village ran through these tunnels. I had some of my engineers trace the river back till they found a band of ashstone."

"Kwai Goo." I look out over the dark jungle, fascinated. "What's it like?"

"What do you mean?"

"Are they really happy there?"

"They might have been," Theodora says. Her shoulders rise and fall, but her sigh is lost in the sound of the wind. "Before the armée came through."

Rage flickers through me, ugly, familiar as the ache of my oldest scars. But Theodora carries the same pain, doesn't she? So do Leo, and Akra . . . even Le Trépas. The country is steeped in it: the pain of choosing between vengeance and forgiveness. Sometimes I envy the dead—after all, souls move on after three days. Then again, they never have a chance to change their minds.

"There it is," Theodora says then. "The cave."

As we bank toward the cliff face, a shadow resolves into the deep mouth of a black cavern. The avion dips, the gleaming waves racing up as though to swallow us. At the last minute, the warbird turns, slipping through a cleft in the sea-swept rocks. If the tide was higher, I'm not sure we would have found it.

We land with a heavy crunch on the broken floor of the cave. Salt air wraps around us; above, a slice of sky gleams through a crack in the earth. The shadows shift as the waves roll in and out, filling tide pools, then sucking them dry, and black crabs and golden souls skitter over the rocks.

Theodora slides from the avion, feet plashing in the shallows. I follow more slowly, my ribs twinging as I find my footing on the slick stone. Opening the storage space at the front of the avion, Theodora pulls out a pack covered in rubber tubing. She slips it onto her back, taking hold of a metal wand attached to the end of the slim tube.

"What is that?" I ask.

"Flamethrower," she says softly, checking the nozzle. I glance around the cavern; the souls are thick around us, but of course Le Trépas is not all we have to fear.

"Do you think there are revenants here?"

With a smile, she flicks the trigger. A burst of fire blooms and fades in the dark. "I hope so. Can you get the other pack, or is it too much to carry?"

Reaching into the belly of the avion, I fish out a canvas

bag that clinks gently as I lift it. The handle of a miner's pick sticks out the top. It isn't heavy, but my side aches when I sling it over my shoulders. Still, I'm not about to complain when the wound is a result of my own actions.

The path twists upward from the pools in a steep set of stairs. I follow Theodora, keeping my eyes on the worn steps. Had the villagers from Kwai Goo carved them to visit the tide pools, gathering seaweed and prying limpets from the rock? No . . . not the villagers. I stop at a switchback, scraping at the algae with the tip of my toe. Carved symbols dance before my eyes, half covered by mud and shadows: the graceful twisting characters of Old Chakran. It was monks who used to carve stories into stone.

"I think there's a temple nearby," I say, my voice echoing in the cavern.

"Temple Fourteen," Theodora replies. "Dedicated to the Keeper of Knowledge."

I stare at her back, but she only continues up the steps. "How do you know that?"

"Luck and legend," she calls back over her shoulder, and I can hear the smile in her voice. "Though this time, the story is Monsieur Audrinne's."

"This is where Le Trépas found the Book of Knowledge?"

I narrow my eyes, peering at the carvings, then up at Theodora. "We aren't really here for the lytheum, are we?"

"Of course we are," she says. "Le Trépas looted the temple almost two decades ago. Anything he didn't take, the armée certainly destroyed. Still, it's interesting. Maybe when this is over, we'll have time to look for the book. To put it back where it belongs and restore what was lost. Come along!"

"When this is over," I repeat, my eyes on my feet as I continue upward. I hadn't given much thought to what would happen after the fight—at least, not in practical terms. My dreams of the future are more like memories of the past: performing with my family, dinners in the comfort of a home that's long gone. What will Chakrana be like when the war is done? What will I be like? Theodora's plan to restore the country is a grand vision, but in my mind's eye, all I can see is our old roulotte, our collection of fantouches, and my family preparing for a show. Will I ever be Jetta of the Ros Nai again, or am I now only a nécromancien?

"Know your enemy," Le Trépas had written, but suddenly I fear I do not know myself as well as I should. I chew my lip, staring at my feet as we climb. The farther we get from the water, the less algae there is on the steps, and the clearer the lettering becomes. Here and there, I can pick out words. *Knowledge*, of course, and *life*, and *death*. Others take more time to puzzle out—*love*, *truth*, and *fear*—after all, I am still a novice in my studies of old Chakran. But as I stand on the steps, another memory comes: the flicker of firelight, the sound of the drum, and shadows dancing on a scrim. "I know this story," I mutter, but Theodora's voice echoes back.

"What was that?"

"I know this story!" I say again, louder this time. But why am I surprised? When the old ways were forbidden, the stories of the gods found new life in the theater. Most shadow plays are versions of myths. "The Keeper and the Liar is carved into the steps!"

"You'll have to tell me sometime," she calls. "For now, save your breath for climbing!"

I look up, and curse. How has she already reached the top? I hurry after her, but the steps seem to multiply as I climb. Soon I am sweating from the exertion as well as the pain in my side. I put my hand against my ribs and press onward, but when I finally catch up, I drop the miner's pack so I can breathe.

Theodora's brow furrows. "Are you all right?"

"It's only a stitch," I say, waving away her concern. My

gesture disturbs the souls that have drifted near. The dead are drawn to my blood; the wound must be bleeding again under the bandage. Theodora gives me a look, but she doesn't bother arguing with me. She takes out her map, pretending to study it while I rest, even though there is only one path ahead.

As my heart slows, a distant sound rises and falls on the breeze. The crash of the waves? The ringing in my ears? No—if I listen close, I can almost pick out a melody. "Do you hear that sound?"

"Over your breathing?" Theodora smiles. "The old stories claim it's the souls whispering their lives to the Keeper of Knowledge, but I'm fairly sure it's just the wind in the lava tunnels."

I return her smile, shaking my head. "How do you know all this?"

"You love performing, but I love learning." She cocks her head as though to listen to the wind. "Wouldn't it be something, to listen to everything everyone has ever known?"

The wind rises, as though to answer her question. The hollow song reminds me of the holy chants Papa used to sing sometimes. He'd learned them in his youth, with the other village children who spent the rainy seasons in the monastery, working the fields and learning to read. When I used to imagine the sound of a hundred voices joining his in harmony, it sounded something like the wind does now.

Had the monks carved the tunnels deeper as well, to catch the wind just so? Or had they heard the song in the wild like a miracle and known this was the place to build their temple? And what had drawn Le Trépas here, two decades ago?

Suddenly I have to see it: the temple dedicated to the Keeper of Knowledge. Knowledge, like the message on the dead man's chest. Grabbing the pack again, I start down the hall, and now it is Theodora hurrying after. "Wait for me!"

We are so close to the surface that the tunnel is more like a rift in the earth, pried open by the water and the wind over the years. Roots and ferns slip through the crack, bringing with them the green, humid scent of the jungle above. By the way the soullight grows steadily brighter, I can tell we're getting close to the temple. Soon enough, I see the broken remains of a carved lintel, with spirits spilling through the doorway like a beacon. I press forward, eager, but Theodora has fallen behind, looking again at her map. "Come back, Jetta!"

Reluctantly, I turn back to see her standing by a branch in the tunnel, the opening as wide as a hungry mouth. How had I missed it?

"The ashstone is just down this hall," she says, but I hesitate. The temple is in the other direction.

I press my hand to my ribs again, pretending the stitch is back, though I can hardly feel the pain anymore. "Go on ahead," I say. "I'll be right behind you."

The concern in Theodora's face almost makes me drop the act. "I can wait."

"It's all right," I say quickly. Then I shrug off the miner's pack. "I just need a minute. The pack is so heavy."

"I can carry it for you—"

"No need," I say, leaning against the wall. "I'll be right behind you."

Theodora frowns, but after a moment, she starts down the tunnel. As soon as she's out of view, I straighten up, jogging lightly back toward the golden doorway.

The light draws me like a moth to a flame. No—not just the light. The temple itself. Le Trépas came here seeking knowledge. I can't shake the feeling that I should do the same—to look for what he had taken, or what he had left behind.

But when I step through the doorway, thoughts of the monk fade. The temple has been carved into a grand cavern in the earth, wider than a paddy, taller than a kapok tree. But roots grow down through the ceiling, and the cracked floor is covered in leaves and rubble. Still, the souls remember that this is a holy place. They soar through the room and scurry over the rubble. The song is louder here as the wind rushes through the chamber like the whispers of the spirits.

Then the skin on the back of my neck prickles, and I whirl. But there is no one else here—no one but the souls. Their glowing light flickers across the high stone walls, illuminating the carvings. Not the usual figures from our stories, nor the stories themselves. Instead, the walls have been chipped into rows and rows of hollows, too regular to be caused by destruction. As I watch the souls duck in and out of the holes, I realize they are empty shelves.

What had been stored here? Offerings? Incense? Knowledge? I remember some of the stories about La Victoire—that the armée had burned thousands of old scrolls. But was it the armée, or Le Trépas?

The skin on the back of my neck crawls again—I feel eyes, I'm sure of it. Turning slowly this time, I scan the room, but I am the only person here. Still, the flickering light casts strange shadows in the rubble. Then I see them— eyes in the carvings on the broken altar. Faces too, or the remains of faces—an ear here, a nose there, the curve of a jawline, the rippled lines of long hair . . . the hundred forms of the Keeper, in their many human lives.

The faces go all the way around the rectangular block of stone. They've been marred with chisels, by the armée or by Le Trépas, and the gems have been pried from their eyes, but I know enough about the Keeper to imagine what used to be. The carvings would have watched the worshippers approach, and listened to their secrets and their dreams. There would have been a bigger statue too, there, behind the altar, though it must have been torn down long ago.

The altar itself is still mostly intact, and though the few others I've seen have been solid, this one is hollow, like a trough . . . or a coffin. There is even a lid, though it has been pushed sideways, exposing whatever was inside. Or is inside.

Is this where the Keeper's book had been? A few quick steps brings me to the altar, but it is only full of dirty water. Disappointed, I trace the carvings on the lip. Life, knowledge, death, repeated all the way around the rim.

Over the smell of the leaves turning slowly to humus, there is still a hint of incense in the air, and flower petals stir on the stone. Even before the armée's defeat, there had been monks who'd come in secret to the temples; shadow plays aren't the only way the old ways have survived. Theodora's words come back to me: perhaps in time, we can restore what was lost.

Theodora . . . how long since I left her in the tunnel? Turning, I start toward the door, then stop short, startled by the glow of an akela standing there.

It shimmers like a column of flame—the soul of a person. I shouldn't be surprised. Souls are drawn to temples, and death, like life, happens every day. But I had not known there were any other people nearby. Just me . . . and Theodora.

My stomach sinks, but then a scream echoes through the tunnels. Her voice. She's alive. "Theodora!"

Breaking into a run, I pelt back the way I'd come. Souls tumble out of my way as I careen down the hall toward the yawning mouth of the tunnel. "Theodora?"

"Jetta! Stay back!" As I start into the darkness, a gout of flame punctuates her shout, bursting from what seems like a crack in the stone. In the sudden brightness, I see another figure standing there. A monk, robed in red, just out of reach of the flames. The firelight shines on the monk's silver hair, but her eyes are sapphire blue.

A n'akela? No—when she sees me, she lifts a gun in her gnarled hand, and despite my many sins, I know I have never done anything to warrant vengeance from this monk. I don't even recognize her. But she recognizes me. "Hello, mei mei," she says. Little sister. "It's good to see you again."

THE KEEPER AND
THE LIAR

In the days when our ancestors were young, the three gods walked among them. The Maiden coaxed new babies to open their eyes, the King collected souls from the dying, and the Keeper gathered all the great and small moments in between, so that no life, no matter how brief, would ever be forgotten.

Then one day, the Keeper met the soul of a liar.

The soul was eager to tell her story: magnificent adventures, endless wealth, true love, and the many grieving children and grandchildren she had left behind. The Keeper listened raptly, but as the hours passed, the King of Death kept tut-tutting, and the Maiden sighed, shaking her head. Annoyed with the interruptions, the Keeper turned to them, curious. "Why do you scoff at her story?"

"Because there was no wealth or love, nor children or grandchildren," the Maiden replied.

The King nodded. "This girl died in her mother's womb."

The Keeper was taken aback, inspecting the soul with new eyes. "Why do you tell me things that aren't true?"

"There is truth in my stories," the soul said. "Not about who I was, but about who we all wish to be."

The Keeper saw the truth of her words. The story was nothing of her life, but all of her soul.

So the Keeper let the liar continue, and three days later, she was still spinning a story as she faded toward her next life. When the last whispers grew too faint for the Keeper to hear, they were stricken with loss. Never before had they not known how a story ended.

So the Keeper plucked up the pieces of the story and scattered them like seeds among the souls nearby. And the Keeper watched eagerly as each soul brought life to this new type of knowledge. The stories changed and grew, creating theories and fantasies and myths and shadow plays, each with a hundred different beginnings, and at least as many endings, and the soul of truth in all of them.

ACT 1,

SCENE 7

In the kitchen of Le Livre—a dim room warm with wood and clay. But the usually tidy space has descended into disarray. The smell of spices and bread is overshadowed with the cloying scent of old rhum. Cups line the sideboard, most of them dirty, and the trash pail is overflowing by the sink.

ELLISIA pulls some dishcloths from a basket, sniffing them delicately before passing them out one by one as the rebels drip water on the kitchen floor. Then she turns back to LEO with a fond look.

ELLISIA: I would hug you, but you smell like river water. Dry off while I fetch you a mop.

LEO *(smiling)*: It's good to see you too, Ellisia. But where's Siris?

ELLISIA: Back in the Lion Lands. He left the minute he saw the deportation decree. He could always read the writing on the wall.

TIA: Did he leave anyone behind, by any chance? Maybe his oldest daughter?

ELLISIA: I wish he had. When I agreed to look out for the inn, I had no idea how much cleaning there'd be. I only used to rent a room here occasionally. Siris never mentioned that men don't pay half so well for clean rooms as for dirty talk. But he said he'd be back as soon as it was safe.

AKRA snorts as he runs the dishcloth over his hair, damp from the rain.

AKRA: That might be some time.

LEO: Sorry, Tia.

She puts on a brave face.

TIA: It's good that she's safe. Besides, I've gotten good at pining.

She turns to CHEEKY, bracing herself for a joke, but the showgirl has a thoughtful look on her face.

CHEEKY: Your name is Ellisia?

She cocks her head, remembering.

You knew Leo's maman.

ELLISIA: So many did, in one way or another. Though she and I met through Leo's father, the old dog. She was always his favorite. I think of her whenever I hear a good chanteuse.

Her sly smile turns sad. She turns back to LEO, gesturing to the violin on his back.

I suppose now isn't the time for a concert, but if you're in town for a while, I hope you'll come and play some of her old songs for me. Perhaps after the *Prix de Guerre* goes, and the rooms are empty again.

CAMREON: The *Prix de Guerre* is actually what brought us here. We want to stop the deportation.

ELLISIA laughs brightly.

ELLISIA: You and all the Aquitans in town. Good luck getting Raik to listen.

CAMREON raises an eyebrow at her tone.

CAMREON: Raik?

ELLISIA: The Boy King.

CAMREON: I know who he is. I'm just surprised to hear you call him by his first name.

ELLISIA folds her arms, her sly smile returning.

ELLISIA: Raik is a long-standing client. We met here at Le Livre, in fact. Quite often.

CAMREON: I see. And have you . . . entertained him since he returned from Le Verdu?

ELLISIA: A lady never tells.

LEO gives her a crooked smile.

LEO: Good thing you're no lady.

ELLISIA laughs, the sound surprisingly raucous.

ELLISIA: Indeed. My girls and I are the only people who've been granted an audience in recent weeks. Raik doesn't even leave the palace anymore. It's driving the Aquitans mad. They're planning a protest in response. Can you imagine? They think that if they gather in the square and shout at the king, he'll listen, but it just makes them easier to shoot.

AKRA: I hope you got them to pay for their rooms in advance.

ELLISIA: Of course I did.

CAMREON: Do you think he plans to respond with force?

ELLISIA: You're asking a lot of questions for a man who's neither paid nor introduced himself.

CAM looks at LEO, who nods once.

CAMREON: I'm Camreon Alendra. Raik is my brother.

ELLISIA's smile freezes.

ELLISIA: I see. I've heard . . . so much about you.

CAMREON: From Raik? What has he said?

ELLISIA: Surely the man who styles himself the rightful king can pay for information.

CAMREON: Alas, I left my treasury in my other pocket.

ELLISIA gives him an arch look.

ELLISIA: Just like a man. Unfortunately, your sour-faced soldier has the right thought.

She jerks a thumb at AKRA, then holds out her hand.

Payment is always in advance.

AKRA glares back at her, but CHEEKY turns to ELLISIA.

CHEEKY: Professional courtesy?

ELLISIA: I let you in, didn't I?

TIA gestures to the tiny diamonds in her ears.

TIA: How about earrings?

ELLISIA tucks her own hair behind her ears, where larger diamonds sparkle.

ELLISIA: I'm not in the market.

LEO: What about that concert?

ELLISIA turns to him, a look of surprise on her face. Then she chuckles again, more quietly this time.

ELLISIA: It's a deal. But if I ask you to play me "The Lights of Lephare" until your fingers cramp, you better not complain.

LEO: Not a word. Only music.

ELLISIA: But not tonight. It's almost dawn. For now, go three blocks over to the Royal Opera House. It's shuttered by royal decree. You should be safe there. I'll come by tomorrow.

CAMREON: Can you give us any information before we go?

ELLISIA: I just did.

She opens the door, ushering them out through it and closing it firmly behind them.

The Lights of Lephare

music and lyrics by
Mei Rath

say you'll take me with you, to see the lights, so splen-did, but

I__ know Le-phare is where she is too.__ In the

light of day, the truth is clear-er, though

I would ra - ther hold on to the lies.

Still, the on - ly way I'll e - ver see Le - phare   Is in the

light   re - flect - ed in your eyes.   They

say the light is bright-er there, you're with me now, de-spite her there, though

some-day we will have to say "Au re - voir." But the

fire of my love will ne-ver die, e-ven though you mean "good-bye," for they

say the light is bright - er in Le -

phare.

CHAPTER EIGHT

Mei mei—little sister. I can tell by the look in the monk's blue eyes that she does not mean it as an honorific. This is no normal revenant, but one of Le Trépas's children—killed at birth, their souls twisted to his service. They survive by slipping from body to rotting body, killing new victims when the flesh begins to fail. I was almost one of them.

Now I back away slowly, keeping my eyes not on the gun in her hand, but on the monk's wizened face. Of course I don't recognize it; she was wearing a different one when I saw her last. "The well outside Hell's Court," I say as the memory floods back—the stinking corpse had dragged me into the mud. "You were there as a dead man."

"Alas," she says, still stepping slowly toward me. "I was there as a dog."

I shudder—the dead dog had stalked us through the tunnels, herding us toward the corpse. . . . Is she doing the same thing now? When the monk takes another step closer, I freeze. On the back of my neck, the hair stands on end.

In one quick motion, I whip the little knife from my belt, drawing it across my palm as I turn. Behind me in the tunnel, the dead man looms. Not the same corpse as back in the well, but the same soul. This body wears armée clothes, crusted with old blood. He lunges for me, but I raise my hand like a threat, and he falls back. Then I turn my head so I can see the monk too. The gun is still in her hand, but her face is uncertain.

At the sight, boldness pushes my fear aside. I tuck my knife back into my belt, and dip my other fingers in my own blood. With one bloody hand facing the dead soldier and the other stretched toward the monk, I take a step closer to her. "If you're going to shoot me, you better do it fast."

"Le Trépas doesn't want you dead," she says quickly, and now she's the one retreating.

"He could have fooled me," I reply as I take another step.

Behind me, the dead soldier follows at a wary distance. "I got his message, by the way. The grenade was a nice touch."

"The message was meant for the Tiger," the monk says. "The moment he offered a truce to the Aquitans was the moment he became our enemy. But to you, Jetta, our father offers an agreement."

"An agreement?" I smirk, taking another step closer. "Let me guess. Wealth? Power?"

"Knowledge," she replies, still retreating. "There's so much he could teach you."

I laugh then, bitter. Le Trépas had offered to teach me once before. He had given me his own blood, and told me to make the symbol of death on a feather to call the soul of a bird. When the soul appeared, blue and vengeful, he'd revealed that I'd ripped it from its new life. "I've already learned my lesson from him."

"Have you learned your history? He remembers the way things were before the Aquitans came and took it all away," the monk says, and now I hesitate. "And he knows how to get it all back."

"To restore what was lost?" The words slip out—I can't help it—and in the tunnels behind me, the wind sighs a distant song.

"Yes." The monk's blue eyes glitter. "You can't imagine the wealth they have—the wealth they have stolen. Even he could hardly believe what he saw in Aquitan. With your help, he can bring it all back to Chakrana."

"I thought he wanted the Aquitans gone," I say.

"That's the start of it," the monk says. "Join him, and he'll even let you keep your moitié."

Leo's face swims behind my eyes. I hate the slur she uses, and the way she speaks, as though he is a pet. But something else caught my attention, and I frown as I take another step down the tunnel. The dead man behind me follows suit. "Le Trépas has been to Aquitan?"

"Do you think his hatred comes from ignorance?" The monk scoffs. "He has seen their selfishness. Their greed. He knows his enemy. You should too."

"I do," I say softly. Then I take a deep breath. "Theodora!"

At my sudden shout, another gout of flame bursts from the crack in the earth, engulfing the dead man behind me; I have led the soldier back to where Theodora is hiding. Flesh burns; hair shrivels. The stench is overwhelming and I gag, but the revenant doesn't so much as scream as he falls, leaving behind the bright blue flame of a n'akela.

The monk is still standing too. I leap at her, bloody

hands outstretched, and she tosses the gun aside to grab my wrists with gnarled fingers.

Grappling, we fall to the floor of the tunnel. "You'll come to him sooner or later," the monk says through her teeth. Her arms shake as I push my own hands inexorably closer to her skin. "Death is inescapable for everyone but him."

She grits her teeth as I make the mark on her wrinkled skin, but when her soul springs free, it is bright gold. I scramble to my feet as the spirit follows its sibling down the hall, but I stumble when I try to follow. My ribs are throbbing, and blood is seeping through the bodice of my borrowed gown.

"Are they gone?" Theodora's voice comes from the crack in the earth.

"Yes."

She peeks out, frowning when she sees me. "Are you okay?"

"Mostly." With a sigh, I sit back down beside the monk's still body. Other souls drift closer, drawn to the blood. In the distant tunnels, the windsong rises and falls: the sound of souls sharing secrets with the Keeper. Has my sister's soul joined them? What secrets would she share?

"Are you sure?" Theodora comes to my side, concern on her face, but I wave her off. Then I grimace at my bloody hands.

"It's worse than it looks," I say. "I'll sit here while you get the lytheum salts."

"I have bad news about that."

Looking up in surprise, I follow her gaze to the cleft in the earth. In the light of the gathering souls, I can make out the marks of picks and chisels. It is not a crack, but a scar. "They took the salts."

"Mined out the whole vein. They must have known we'd come looking for it at some point."

"But where did they take it all?" Then I curse as the answer comes. "Nokhor Khat."

"That's my guess, though of course it's hard to ask." Glaring, she nudges the monk's corpse with her foot. The sight shocks me.

"Don't!" My voice echoes in the tunnel, and Theodora startles, wide-eyed. I open my mouth, looking for the words to explain. "His minions—these n'akela . . . he made them what they are. And now they're only following orders. Besides, it isn't even her body," I add, remembering the akela I'd seen in the temple. "She killed a monk to get it.

I saw the monk's real soul by the altar. She may have been trying to warn me."

Theodora narrows her eyes, looking from me to the body, then back. "You went to the temple."

"It's just down the hall," I say, defensive, but she turns back to the body.

"And the monk's soul is there?"

"She was," I say, frowning. "Why?"

"Well." She kneels down beside the body, tucking a strand of silver hair behind the old monk's ear. "Le Trépas can't be the only one who remembers the way things were before La Victoire."

"You want me to bring her back?" I look askance at Theodora, then back to the body. I have made many fantouches out of smaller souls, but the only times I've trapped akela, it had been under duress. Sunan . . . or Akra. "It seems disrespectful."

"We only need her to answer a few questions," Theodora says. "And isn't that at the heart of the Keeper's powers? Passing down knowledge?"

I chew my lip, staring at the monk, but now I too am curious. She might even remember when Le Trépas came to the temple. And if there was a way to stop the nécromancien, wouldn't the Keeper's monk want to share it?

Slowly, carefully, Theodora and I lift the old monk's body and carry her back to the soul-bright temple. Without the n'akela inhabiting her skin, the body is fragile, light—the bones like a bird's. With her own soul looking on, we lay the monk's body down gently by the altar where she would have worshipped, near the faded flowers she herself might have put there.

Then, as respectfully as possible, I make the mark of life on her forehead. With a soft gasp, she opens her eyes, and I am relieved to see they are as dark as tea.

"This is . . ." Her voice is a whisper as air returns to her lungs. "Unseemly."

"I'm sorry, grandmother," I say, but Theodora is already pulling a notebook from her pockets. I have seen it before—or one much like it. She keeps them everywhere.

Flipping past doodles and notes and diagrams, she finds a blank page, then pulls out a pen. "Have you heard of the Keeper's Book of Knowledge?"

The monk only purses her lips, giving the Aquitan girl a look. "Answer her questions, please," I say, softening the order, and the monk's mouth twists.

"Of course I have."

Theodora wets her lips. "Do you know where it is?"

The monk gives her a pointed look. "If I did, I would have put it back where it belongs."

I glance over my shoulder, at the broken altar, filled with stagnant water. "If we find it, we'll do just that."

The monk turns her head, slowly, painfully, and in the soullight I can see bruises around her neck. "If you find it," she repeats. "Le Trépas hid it well before the armée imprisoned him."

"Do you have any idea where?" Theodora asks, but the monk shrugs.

"Those of us who remain have been searching the countryside for years," she replies. "It is nowhere to be found."

Dread creeps into Theodora's voice. "Could he have destroyed it?"

"No," the monk says simply. "Or their soul would have been reborn."

"Whose soul?"

"The Keeper's." The monk reaches out to the altar, resting her gnarled hand on the stone. "Do you know the story? How they took human form to learn what life was. How they were born, and died, and born again a thousand times. The book is bound in their holy skin," she says. "And it holds their soul. It has not been destroyed."

I do know the story—it's part of our troupe's repertoire. But Theodora looks up from the page, a delicate look on her face. I know what she's thinking. Is what the monk says true, or only wishful thinking? "Are you sure?" she says at last, and the monk fixes her with a solemn look.

"I am," she says. "Because when I died, no one came to hear my story."

Theodora's hand stills on the page. On the breeze, the wind sings. "Did you expect to see the Keeper?"

"Of course I did. If the book had been destroyed, the Keeper's soul would have been there. If the book was close by, I would have seen their faces. Instead I saw nothing. The Keeper is not in Chakrana."

"Not in Chakrana," Theodora repeats slowly, tapping her pen on the page, but when I meet her eyes, I know she's thinking the same thing I am.

"When did Le Trépas go to Aquitan?" I ask her.

Theodora cocks her head, but it is the monk who answers. "It was after he took the book," she says. "Aquitan is one place we have not been able to search."

Theodora stands, pacing through the temple, careless

of the souls that swirl around her feet. "Thank you, grandmother," I say to the monk, but she only bows her head.

"All the thanks I want is to be released," she says. "And that you burn my body, so this doesn't happen again."

I frown, taken aback. "But . . . what about your story? Without the Keeper, it won't be heard."

"Life must go on," she says. "As must death. As for the knowledge in between, I will create it anew someday."

She raises a hand to her forehead, rubbing away the mark I had made. Then she sits down beside the altar, her back against the stone, and beckons me closer. Taking my bloody hand in her own, she traces the mark of death on her own skin. Her body sags sideways as her soul bursts free.

Gently I lay the monk's wrinkled hand in her lap, stepping back just as Theodora turns from her pacing. "We have to go to Aquitan," she says, but I had already guessed she would say so.

"We came here for the elixir," I remind her.

She raises an eyebrow. "There's elixir at Les Chanceux."

I chew my lip, but in truth, I cannot muster many other objections. Our friends are in Nokhor Khat, and the fight there still draws me, but Le Trépas lurks behind it all like a shadow. If he wants me to come to the capital, even I know it is wiser to stay away and to gather what knowledge we can.

Before we leave the temple, we grant the monk's last request. Theodora empties the accelerant from the reservoirs of the flamethrower, and we burn the corpse as the akela looks on. Then, as the wind in the tunnels clears the smoke, we return to the avion.

By the time we reach the bottom of the stairs, the tide has begun to rise around the warbird's bronze feet, and she shakes the salt spray from her wings as she takes to the dawn sky. As the shore of my country fades into the distance, my heart is racing again—not with the thrill of flight, but the thrill of what's over the horizon.

ACT 2

FOLLOWING

the Boy King's shocking
and unlawful demand
for the removal of all foreigners
from Chakrana,

we say:

*We may have come
as strangers,
but we will stay as friends.
As soldiers and public servants.
As merchants and traders.*

We will not go.

❌ ❌ ❌

VIVE
LES CHAKRATANS

❌ ❌ ❌

ACT 2,

SCENE 9

Afternoon in the Royal Opera House. The previous king commissioned it in imitation of the one in Lephare, but the Aquitan-style decor doesn't hold up to Chakran humidity. The brass chandeliers are tarnished, and there is a musty smell in the red velvet curtains. The stage is still set for the last show: a romance performed in celebration of the Boy King's coronation. Now dust gathers on the wide boards, and the painted backdrop is fading; the air that once shook with laughter and applause is still and stale but for the gentle sound of LEO's violin.

   He sits cross-legged on the stage, plucking at the strings of the instrument in his lap. Every few notes, he stops to pull the pencil from behind his ear and scribble on the sheaf of staff paper beside him. TIA and CHEEKY look on from the audience as they share a jar of pickled eggs. Both girls have clearly found the costume shop, taking the opportunity to change out of their damp trousers and into ruffled dresses, along with, in TIA's case, a lush auburn wig.

TIA: You know I love your music, Leo, but if you're hungry, you better hurry. Cheeky is eating all the pickled eggs.

LEO: I just want to finish the chorus.

He plucks out another few notes.

CHEEKY: Are you going to play it for Ellisia?

LEO: No.

LEO chuckles as he marks the notes on the page.

It's a love song.

CHEEKY turns to TIA.

CHEEKY: Maybe Tia can sing it to her, then.

TIA: I told you, Ellisia is not the girl I meant. The innkeeper's daughter is tall and graceful. With the darkest skin and eyes like . . . like . . .

CHEEKY: Pickled eggs?

TIA takes off her wig and throws it at CHEEKY, who cackles. AKRA lifts his head from the back of the velvet chair. The armée cap he found in the costume shop falls away from his face.

AKRA: Some of us are trying to get some rest.

TIA: I thought you didn't need to sleep.

AKRA: I wouldn't if you all weren't so exhausting.

Lifting the cap once more, he puts it back over his eyes. Then he snatches it away and stands, his hand going to his gun at the sound of the theater door creaking.

Who's there?

CAMREON *(offstage)*: It's only me.

AKRA relaxes as CAM appears at the end of the aisle, one of the protest flyers in his hand.

Has Ellisia come by?

CHEEKY: We're still waiting. What's that?

CAMREON approaches, holding out the flyer. CHEEKY takes it, puzzling out the Aquitan words.

CAMREON: It's posted everywhere downtown.

CHEEKY: Do they actually think it will work?

CAMREON: If I was Raik, I would respond.

CHEEKY: What if you were Le Trépas?

CAMREON makes a face.

CAMREON: The response would be a little different. But with the palace locked up tight and guards at all the doors, it's my best chance to see Raik in person.

His hand drifts to his pocket, as though to confirm that the fountain pen containing Jetta's blood is still close at hand.

With any luck, this will be over in a few hours.

TIA raises an eyebrow, then turns to CHEEKY.

TIA: Give me back my wig, will you? If I'm going to die surrounded by Aquitans, at least let me do it with good hair.

A smile ghosts across CAMREON's face.

CAMREON: Akra and I will be going alone. A larger group of Chakrans would call too much attention. Besides, I need someone to stay here and wait for Ellisia.

AKRA sighs as he stands, brushing the wrinkles out of the costume-shop uniform, and LEO looks up from his violin.

LEO: I'm coming too. To look for my brother.

CAMREON: Xavier isn't your brother anymore, no more than Raik is mine. And if something goes wrong, I expect the rest of you to pull us out of the fire. You still have your supply of blood?

LEO draws the fountain pen out of his pocket with a flourish.

Good. If we're not back by nightfall, I'd appreciate it if you came looking. If Ellisia does show up, ask her to wait till we return.

TIA: She'll charge by the hour.

CAMREON: We'll go as fast as we can.

TIA: That's what they all say.

AKRA chuckles as they slip out of the theater, but CHEEKY watches them go, her face troubled. When she hears the door click shut, she turns to LEO, who is already packing up his violin.

CHEEKY: We're following them, aren't we?

LEO: Of course not.

He jumps off the edge of the stage onto the dusty carpet.

They'll see us if we try, and we already know where they're going. We'll take the long way to the plaza.

MAP OF
LEPHARE
CAPITAL OF AQUITAN

1. Palais du Roi
2. Cathedral
3. Royal Opera
4. Warehouses
5. Docks
6. Les Chanceux

CHAPTER

TEN

It is past sunset by the time we see Lephare glimmering on the horizon. Like Nokhor Khat, the capital of Aquitan sits at the mouth of a river that flows into the Hundred Days Sea, but as we approach, the differences become much clearer.

Instead of the organic sweep of the streets in Chakrana, this city grows outward from the docks in a strange geometry—almost crystalline, with straight roads that break suddenly around gemlike buildings. At home, the nights are lit by a patchwork of torches and lanterns, cookfires and electric bulbs, but here, lamps line the thoroughfares at regular intervals—fire and glass, like the souls of diamonds. In Chakrana, roofs are made of thatch or colorful tile that turns up at the eaves, but the buildings in Lephare are topped with steely slate, like stone scales, and it seems that every window is covered not with carved screens or shutters, but glass.

Is it to keep out the chill? The night air here is so different from the warm humidity I am used to. Now the long sleeves of my borrowed Aquitan dress make more sense. I wrap my arms around myself as we circle the city. "Are you looking for a place to land?" I say at last, shivering, but Theodora shakes her head.

"I'm counting the ships in the harbor." She points at a veritable forest of masts and smokestacks. "There are more than enough to safely transport the refugees from Chakrana."

"Xavier must have told your uncle that the *Prix de Guerre* was sufficient," I say, but she shakes her head.

"He may have," she says. "But my uncle should know better than that."

"Le Roi Fou—the Mad King?" I say, raising an eyebrow, but Theodora gives me a look.

"You should know that the malheur you share doesn't make you forget facts."

"Not exactly," I agree. "But it can make you ignore them. Maybe it's wishful thinking."

"We'll know soon enough, I suppose." Theodora's frown is skeptical, but as she turns the avion away from the docks, my heart quickens. I must admit, I am eager to meet the Mad King of Aquitan. All I know about him are the stories I've been told—his love of shadow plays, his use of Les Chanceux. What is he like in person, this man who openly shares my malheur, who has found a way to manage it, along with an entire kingdom? When Theodora points at a cluster of grand buildings along the curve of the river, I lean out of the avion to get a better look. "There it is," she says. "The palais du roi."

I cock my head, trying to make sense of the profusion of slate roofs and tall chimneys ahead. How can Theodora pick it out? "I thought you hadn't been here in years."

"I'm a general's daughter," she says. "I've studied the maps."

"I've only seen the paintings," I say, but as we approach the city center, another building catches my eye, wreathed in smokeless flame.

It is the cathedral of Lephare, illuminated by the fire of a thousand souls. Light flickers around the famed spire and gleams through a stained-glass window bigger than a rice barn. As we swoop closer, I can see that every glass pane is intact, as are all the carvings—monstrous faces and men in robes with flowers at their feet. I stare, half in awe, half in jealousy. I have never seen a temple so unspoiled.

But as we pass over the cathedral, light gives way to shadow in a pit like a scar on the earth. Along a low wall that edges the street, mounds of dank soil are piled high and scattered with shovels and barrows and broken boards. "What's that?" I say, pointing—the muddy hole seems so out of place in the city center.

"It looks like one of my uncle's public health initiatives," Theodora says as we circle lower. "He's excavating the boneyards across the city center."

"Boneyards?" I shudder at the thought of planting the dead in the earth, like rotting fruit. "You mean graves?"

"Thousands of them," Theodora confirms. "Lephare is an old city, with far more dead than living. Whenever it rains, bodies practically climb from the cemeteries. My uncle often complained about the smell in his letters," she adds, and my stomach turns at the memory of the dead man in the rice paddy. "I actually suggested once that he burn them, but apparently the priests found the idea blasphemous. So I told him to move them instead."

I look at her askance. "He has time to move the dead but not the living?"

"The dead raised a bigger stink," she says with a wry smile. "At least, until now."

Past the cathedral, I can finally get a clear look at the palais: an enormous limestone building erected around a central courtyard, facing the cathedral. The shape of it is unfamiliar, but the layout reminds me of Hell's Court, with the Ruby Palace nearby. All the seats of power, close together—where the gods can watch the kings, and vice versa.

As the bird drops lower, I see we already have an audience. Even at this late hour, there are people watching us, their pale faces shining like small moons in the light of the gas lamps. The courtyard spreads below us like a stage, but my stomach drops as Theodora pulls up again to circle. Why wait to land? Ah—as I watch, the crowd swells, with courtiers and servants alike rushing out from inside the palais. La Fleur takes us around once more in a slow descent, giving the gathering time to grow. I am cold and tired, but I admire her commitment to showmanship.

The avion touches down at last, bronze claws scraping

the granite cobbles. Metal grinds on metal as the warbird folds her wings. When Theodora steps to the plaza, her golden curls gleaming in the light, the Aquitans greet her with applause. But to me, their cheers sound like distant screams.

Would anyone in Chakrana run toward a war machine? Perhaps the Aquitans don't realize how much they have to fear—at least, not yet. A dark impulse rises in me: the same feeling I had when Fontaine's men arrived at the coronation with a bloody prisoner in tow. I want to teach them what fear is. But this time Leo isn't watching me. I have to watch myself.

Taking a deep breath, I follow Theodora out of the avion. After so many hours in the air, there is an ache in my legs that echoes the dull pain in my ribs. But I stand up straighter as the impromptu audience parts around a tall man. The crown gives him away—no simple carved circlet, but a lacy dome of gold topped with a sapphire the size of a human heart. He wears layers of silk and velvet; his broad shoulders are covered with a robe trimmed in spotted fur. But beneath the outlandish clothing, his features are oddly familiar. The silver hair, the hawkish nose . . . if he'd been wearing an armée uniform, I could have mistaken him for his half-brother, the first General Legarde.

His appearance throws me; it's like looking into the face of a dead man—one who I killed. But Theodora calls to him warmly. "Uncle!"

"My dear niece," Le Roi says, reaching out to the girl, and I know enough Aquitan to understand him. He clasps her hands, kissing her on both cheeks, then drawing back to study her face. "Your portrait hardly does you justice. I'm so relieved you took my advice and left Chakrana."

"I'll be going back as soon as your three fastest ships are ready to come with me," Theodora says, pitching her voice to carry. The crowd around us murmurs at her boldness. But now I know why she wanted an audience—it makes her so much harder to ignore. "I would never abandon Chakrana, but many Aquitans must, and they must do so safely."

"There is already a ship in Nokhor Khat waiting to bring our people home," the king replies, still smiling, though his expression has hardened like amber.

"The *Prix de Guerre*?" The surprise on Theodora's face is pretense. "A cargo ship can't safely transport so many passengers."

"Your own brother feels differently," the king says, loud enough for the assembled court to hear. "The general d'armée sends me regular updates on his preparations. As does the Boy King, who has promised to outfit the ship for the journey."

"I wouldn't trust either of them," I interject, enunciating carefully, aware of how my accent inflects the Aquitan words. To my surprise, Theodora's hand shoots out, as though to stop me from saying more. But I have already caught the king's attention.

He takes me in with a glance that sweeps from my windblown hair to my stolen shoes. "And who are you?"

The crowd turns, curious, and for a moment, I see myself through their eyes. Madame's dress, so fine in Chakrana, is clearly years out of date here in Lephare, not to mention ill-fitting and stained with blood. And of all the people assembled in the square, I am the only one without Aquitan features. If I were in the audience, I might assume Theodora had brought a poorly dressed servant along with her. I draw myself up—if the king had reports from the armée, surely he would know my name. "I'm Jetta Chantray."

"Ah," the king says, and now he looks impressed. "The shadow player."

The crowd murmurs again, but I cock my head. Despite his well-known love of shadow plays, that is not what I'd expected Le Roi to focus on. Still, I can still see Theodora's warning hand out of the corner of my eye, so all I do is bow. "Your Majesty."

"With the unrest in Chakrana, I fear you may be the last shadow player I ever meet," the king says, with a wistful look on his face. "Welcome, Jetta. But you must be tired from your journey," he adds then, turning back to Theodora. "We'll have refreshments in the hall of mirrors. Come!"

At his invitation, a handful of servants rush back toward the palais to make ready. The king too starts across the square, though he moves with much less haste. When he offers Theodora his right arm, she takes it. Then, to my surprise, he offers me the other.

In Chakrana, most strangers hesitate to touch a nécromancien. Is it possible the king doesn't know what I am? Or is he only trying to keep the crowd from being frightened? The Aquitans whisper as I slip my hand through the crook of his elbow. The velvet trim of his shirt is as soft as petals.

Crossing the wide plaza, the courtiers step out of our way, and the great arched doors of the palais open before us. Or rather, before Le Roi. From the ground, the building is even more impressive than it was from above. It looms over us in pale limestone and glittering glass, the stately colonnades stretching several stories high. Stepping inside, my feet sink ankle-deep into a rich carpet as purple as a field of indigo in bloom. It must have taken at least as many blossoms to dye so much thread. Vaulted ceilings soar overhead, stamped with intricate plasterwork, and art lines the walls. Madame Audrinne's home seems like a hovel by comparison.

The king catches me staring, and his eyes gleam, the same color as the stone in his crown. "Do tell me you'll stay long enough to give a performance," he says hopefully. "I was devastated to hear of the rebel attack on the Fêtes des Ombres."

I blink as the memories resurface. The festival was held every year: a celebration of shadow plays, where Le Roi's brother had chosen the best troupe to sponsor for a trip to Aquitan. "I was there when the stage exploded," I say softly. Then I frown, hearing voices behind us like an echo. Half turning, I see the courtiers following us down the hall. I glance at Theodora, raising my eyebrows, but she shakes her head almost imperceptibly, and the king himself ignores the crowd at our heels.

"That must have been terrifying," he replies. "Had you come to perform at the festival?"

"We had," I say, trying to remember what show we'd meant to do. The Shepherd and the Tiger, wasn't it? A show meant to flatter the late general in hopes he would take notice despite the modest size of our troupe. All we would have needed was a moment of his attention, but we had never even gotten to the stage. "My troupe was . . . is . . . one of a kind. We put on shadow plays without sticks or strings."

"Now *that* I'd like to see," the king says, but on his other side, Theodora places a gentle hand on his arm.

"There are more important concerns than shadow plays, uncle."

"Blasphemy," the king says with a grin, leading us through a tall arched doorway. A servant stands on either side. Their pale faces are unsettling: I am unused to seeing Aquitans in servants' livery. At the king's gesture, they close the heavy double door behind us, leaving the gaggle of disappointed courtiers on the other side of it.

In an instant, the king's easy smile twists, and he shrugs us off to stalk toward the seating area. "Nevertheless, my *dear* niece," he calls back to Theodora, the words much more pointed now. "Come and tell me why you've tried to embarrass me in public."

His footsteps echo crisply across the inlaid floor, each step punctuating his displeasure. I glance at Theodora, unmoored, but her own expression is as hard as the marble tiles.

She starts after him, and I follow. The room is impossibly long, with more than a dozen arched windows looking out over a vast garden to the south. The opposite wall is lined with hundreds of mirrors, and the silvered glass—such a luxury!—reflects my image back to me like a mockery. I am bedraggled and out of place. When I reach the plush velvet couches, I hesitate to touch the soft cloth in my stained gown, but Theodora takes a seat opposite the king as though she had invited him.

"My goal is not to embarrass you, uncle," she says firmly, though the way she'd made the avion circle above the growing crowd belies her claim. "My goal is to prevent a humanitarian crisis."

"Alas, the deportation seems inevitable after your brother's defeat in Le Verdu," the king replies. "I have written to the Boy King, but he will not rescind his order. He has lost trust in the armée's ability to protect his best interests against the rebellion, and so like many failed rulers, he is turning to populism to try to appease his people."

"It isn't inevitable," Theodora says. "The rightful king is still trying to stop the deportation."

"The rebel prince?" With an amused expression, the king leans forward to study the food laid out on the low table between us: delicate morsels of pastry, pungent cheese, and dried fruit scattered like gems on the tray. "I wish him better luck than he's had ascending the throne."

Theodora doesn't take the bait. "If the Aquitans must be deported, let them go safely on ships meant for passengers."

"The *Prix de Guerre* leaves in . . . two days, is it?" The king selects a tartlet. "Even my fastest ships couldn't get to Chakrana in time."

"I agree that it would have been preferable to send them sooner," Theodora replies pointedly. "But with lives at stake, we must do all we can with the time we have. If you send them tonight, they can still meet the *Prix de Guerre* halfway."

"My ships are bound for other ports," the king says, taking a bite of the tart. The buttery crust flakes like nacre over his lap. "Our interests in Chakrana are not our only holdings, and far from our most profitable ones, these days. I swore months ago that the *Prix de Guerre* would be the last ship I sent to Chakrana."

"Profit and promises mean nothing to Le Trépas!" The

words tumble out of me—Le Roi's reasoning makes me furious. Theodora shoots me another look, but I have to make her uncle understand. "He's the one behind all of this, Your Majesty."

"Le Trépas?" The king laughs, his voice tinged with scorn. "The great Chakran boogeyman. Someone can't trip in Chakrana without it being Le Trépas's fault. I must confess, I have no idea how such an unremarkable man became so feared, but I suppose superstition is native to your people." He finishes the tart, then waves at the tray. "Try these, they're very good."

"Le Trépas—unremarkable?" I blink, taken aback, but Theodora interjects smoothly.

"You met him once, didn't you?"

"Years ago. Of course, he was only known as Kuzhujan back then." The king butchers the name as he reaches for a piece of cheese. "That was when he was still hungry for an alliance between us."

"An alliance?" I am no politician, but it is hard to imagine Le Trépas wanting to ally himself with Le Roi. "Wasn't there already one in place?"

"Between the King of Chakrana and myself, yes," Le Roi says. "Unfortunately, the monk found the king's rule too secular for his taste. Le Trépas felt he could do a better job on the throne, so he asked for my help ending the Alendra line. Of course, as Theodora knows, I cannot lend my support to an upstart," Le Roi says with a pointed look at his niece. "No matter what he offers in return."

It is clearly a barb—why doesn't Theodora defend Camreon? Especially knowing that Le Roi had in fact ordered the deaths of King Alendra and his family, only to blame the murders on Le Trépas. The truth burns on my tongue, but Theodora's careful expression reminds me to school my own. Politics is clearly a stage I am not yet used to, and I do not know my lines.

Leaning across the table, Theodora speaks softly. "What did Le Trépas offer you, uncle?"

"Oh, his gifts were quite princely," the king says, inclining his head so the sapphire in his crown catches the light. A Chakran sapphire. What god's eye had it once adorned? Still Theodora does not lose her focus.

"Did he give you anything else? A book, perhaps? It's a traditional gift in Chakrana," she lies smoothly. "Sometimes the contents are intended to be meaningful."

The king laughs. "Fitting that the book was blank. Perhaps Le Trépas was smarter than he seemed."

"Blank?" I frown—that can't be right. "Can I see it?"

The king cocks his head at me, puzzled. "Why?"

"Superstition," I shoot back, but he narrows his eyes.

"You must eschew such things," Le Roi says, taking another piece of cheese from the tray. "They don't do you or your people any favors. Especially in your new life in Lephare."

"Lephare? No, uncle," Theodora reminds him firmly. "As I said before, we're going back, and I strongly request you reconsider sending ships. I don't know what my . . . what the general has written to you, but Jetta is right. I don't think his reports can be trusted."

"Why not, Theodora?" The king's expression softens, as though for the first time he is seeing his niece and not a fellow politician—or a rival. "You and Xavier used to hold each other in high regard."

"There are . . . forces at work in Chakrana," Theodora says carefully. "Forces that are difficult to explain. The book itself might shed some light on the matters. It's one reason I came to speak to you in person."

The king is still watching her with sympathy in his eyes. "What forces do you mean?"

Theodora hesitates, glancing at me, then back at the

king. "There may be more to Chakran superstition than we used to think."

Le Roi frowns at her, then at the cheese he's holding. "This is troubling, Theodora," he says, putting the cheese back on the tray. Then he brushes the crumbs from his lap and onto the thick carpet. "Let me think about what to do. We'll discuss it further in the morning."

"Another favor, uncle," Theodora says as the king stands. "Jetta suffers from the same malady you do, though of course we don't have Les Chanceux in Chakrana. I was hoping you'd be willing to give us some elixir."

"Elixir?" The king looks from her, to me, then back. "That is a simpler request. I'm happy to grant it in exchange for a shadow play."

"A play?" I bite my lip, frustrated—this should have been an easy bargain, but I haven't put on a show in months now, and I am far from prepared. "All of my fantouches are back in Chakrana, Your Majesty."

"I have an extensive collection to choose from," he says, waving away my concerns. "I keep my best ones in the Salon des Merveilles."

The words take me a moment to translate. "The Room of Wonders?"

"One of my treasuries. The book is there too," he adds with a significant look at Theodora. "I can show you tomorrow, if you'd like."

"Tomorrow, then," Theodora agrees, though I can see the impatience in her eyes. The king only smiles.

"If you're as good as you say, Jetta, I'll send you home with a ship as well, to carry your supply." Le Roi gestures to the servants still standing by the hall, and they swing the doors open wide. I am eager to speak to Theodora in private, but to my surprise, the courtiers are still waiting outside, peering at us through the open doorway. "Show my guests to the Chakran suite," Le Roi adds, and the servants race to obey. "And fetch them a flask of the water from Les Chanceux!"

I stiffen as a dozen voices echo his words: Les Chanceux, Les Chanceux. The courtiers must know what the water is for. Will they be speculating about me? About my malheur? The king might be cavalier about signing his own madness into his name, but of course he could afford to be. As the servant leads us through the crowd, I can feel eyes following me. When we finally turn down an empty hall, I have never been so relieved to be rid of an audience.

ACT 2,

SCENE 11

The square outside the Ruby Palace. In better days, visitors of state would parade past the tall stone statues—dragons and tigers, leaders and heroes, and birds that rise fully fledged from the gilded shells of stone eggs—and up the wide steps, where the carved doors, ten feet high, would be pushed open on silent hinges by guards in red uniforms.

Now the doors are shut tightly, and the guards are nowhere to be seen. Instead, Aquitans pack the square. Businessmen. Sugar barons. Plantation owners. Not men used to waiting on the wrong side of a locked door.

Some hold copies of the Boy King's recent decree—the demand that all Aquitans leave the city on the next ship. Others have a different letter in their hands: the flyer making the case that all "Chakratans" must stay. It is an unfamiliar position to them. Never before had they considered they might not belong.

As CHEEKY and LEO skirt the edges of the plaza, the Aquitans eye them, suspicious. CHEEKY blows a kiss at a man in a suit, who glares and turns away. The showgirl sticks her tongue out at his back.

CHEEKY: I hate crowds.

LEO: You love crowds.

CHEEKY: I hate *this* crowd.

LEO: You can still go back to the opera house.

His tone is earnest, but she bristles.

CHEEKY: And leave you and Akra without any moral support?

She winks at another Aquitan businessman.

Or immoral support, as the case may be. But when they're looking at me, they're not looking at you.

Indeed, the Aquitans who eye LEO for his mixed features turn away quickly when CHEEKY returns their brazen stares. LEO ignores all of them, craning his neck to scan the crowd.

LEO: Do you see him?

CHEEKY: They're up near the front.

CHEEKY points toward the steps of the palace, where AKRA and CAMREON lurk half hidden behind the statue of a dragon. LEO shakes his head.

LEO: I meant Xavier.

CHEEKY: Oh. Not yet. But—

Before she can finish her sentence, a shout rings out across the plaza.

AUDRINNE: Vive les Chakratans! Vive les Chakratans!

A ripple goes through the crowd as a carriage arrives, all polished ebony and gold detailing. BERTRAND AUDRINNE himself stands in the driver's seat, wearing not a plantation suit but an old armée uniform, and chanting with the élan of someone half his age.

The crowd parts, cheering, as the horses stride to the center of the plaza. AUDRINNE reaches out as he sees familiar faces in the crowd.

AUDRINNE: Charles, so good to see you again. Albert, how is your cousin? Send her my best.

As AUDRINNE shakes hands, AKRA nudges CAMREON. Then he points to the back of the carriage, where a small boy stares out with frightened eyes.

AKRA: What kind of fool brings his child to a fight?

CAMREON: He might not expect a fight.

AKRA: Then he's forgotten his time in the armée.

AKRA jerks his chin toward the rooftop of the Ruby Palace, where guards in red peer over the upswept eaves. Here and there, the afternoon sun glints off the barrels of their rifles. But CAMREON shakes his head.

CAMREON: I think he remembers it too well. The armée he knew would never hurt an Aquitan.

Reaching the steps, AUDRINNE yanks the reins, and the horses bluster as the carriage rolls to a stop. Turning to scan the crowd, AUDRINNE raises a hand to quell the chanting.

AUDRINNE: My compatriots! My fellows! My friends. It gives me heart to stand with you today!

A scattered cheer goes up, but AUDRINNE brings his hand to his chest.

How I wish it were under better circumstances.

The crowd mutters as AUDRINNE draws a paper from his pocket. Unfolding it, he shows it to the crowd: the deportation decree.

"All foreigners must report to the capital for deportation." Simple words for a rallying cry. But as a policy, so hard to understand. What is a foreigner, here in Nokhor Khat, where an Aquitan fort guards the harbor and our armée guards her people? What is a foreigner when most of Chakrana's business is done through Aquitans, and Aquitan currency is used? I may have been born in Aquitan, but I have lived in Chakrana for more years than the Boy King has been alive. I am more familiar with the paddies than the plaza of Lephare. Can I truly be called a foreigner?

AUDRINNE pauses for the crowd to answer. Their responses drift to his waiting ears—"No!" Then he returns to the flyer.

"All foreigners must report to the capital." But who are we to report to? The palace is shut tight, and the Boy King has refused any audiences. Perhaps because he knows he cannot explain his decree. I would ask him, am I a foreigner? Are we?

AUDRINNE points at his friends in the crowd.

Charles—you work in imports. You provide jobs at your warehouses, not to mention brandy and fine clothing to all of us locals. Albert, you own several silk plantations in the mountains, and the economy there relies on your business. And in La Sucrier, my fields and my wife are waiting for me to come home.

The thought makes the crowd stir again. Not all of them have lived in Chakrana as long as AUDRINNE, but they have all carved a place for themselves here—some of them with knives. As AUDRINNE looks out over their heads, he catches sight of LEO.

What of the moitié? Is he a foreigner too? Where will he go?

AUDRINNE points, and the crowd turns to gawk at him. LEO stiffens, putting his head down, but CAMREON has already seen him. He swears under his breath.

AKRA: You can say that again.

Standing on tiptoe, he meets CHEEKY's eye across the crowd and mouths the words.

Go back to the theater!

CHEEKY replies with the same exaggerated expressions.

CHEEKY: Make me!

Now AKRA is the one to swear. CAMREON waves him off.

CAMREON: Go. Get them out of here.

AKRA nods, pushing through the crowd and working his way around the square. But AUDRINNE has already turned back to his audience.

How can any of us be foreigners when we are a vital part of Chakrana? How can the Boy King expect us to abandon our responsibilities? Chakrana depends on us. Our businesses, our management, our money. If we go back to Aquitan, it all goes with us! And so I stand with you, to declare our right to stay.

The crowd murmurs as AUDRINNE draws the silver pistol from his belt, and the afternoon sun gleams on the epaulets on his old uniform.

And if the Boy King thinks otherwise, he must tell us to our faces why we do not belong!

Marching up the steps of the Ruby Palace, AUDRINNE uses the butt of the gun to knock on the door. The sound echoes in the hall beyond, but there is no answer from inside.

Meanwhile, AKRA continues around the restless crowd, as CAM checks his pocket once again for the pen filled with blood.

The crowd too is waiting for the Boy King. AUDRINNE raises his pistol and knocks again. As he steps back, the door begins to creak open at last. The crowd presses closer, but it is GENERAL LEGARDE who steps out from the palace.

LEO's face goes pale. He grabs CHEEKY's hand.

LEO: That's Xavier.

When AUDRINNE sees LEGARDE, the man smiles tightly.

AUDRINNE: General. I am Lieutenant Bertrand Audrinne, and I am here to see the king.

LEGARDE looks at him with bright blue eyes, and his voice is pitched to carry over the crowd.

LEGARDE: The king is not accepting visitors. Now please. All Aquitans must report to the *Prix de Guerre*.

The crowd mutters, and AUDRINNE is taken aback. LEO's own face falls, though it is hard to tell if he is disappointed or relieved.

LEO: No . . . not Xavier.

CHEEKY: How can you tell?

LEO: His accent. Xavier's own Aquitan was flawless.

CHEEKY squeezes his hand, trying to comfort him. Then she spies AKRA making his way toward them.

CHEEKY: Akra's coming to scold us. Should we go back to the theater?

LEO: Not yet.

He cranes his neck to keep an eye on XAVIER as AUDRINNE draws himself up.

AUDRINNE: As an officer and a veteran, I demand the Boy King explain how he can turn his back on us.

LEGARDE: It is not your place to ask for an explanation from the king.

AUDRINNE's eyes widen; he is incensed.

AUDRINNE: My place? My place is in my sitting room,

enjoying my brandy. Which I could do if you had known your own place and held the line. In fact . . .

The rest of his objection is lost in the sudden murmur that ripples through the crowd. The palace door is opening again, and a cold voice drifts out.

RAIK: Alas, your place is in fact aboard the *Prix de Guerre*.

Hidden behind the statue, CAMREON tenses as his own brother walks through the door. The last time he'd seen RAIK, the Boy King was lying motionless and bloody outside Le Trépas's empty cell. Now RAIK looks pale and sallow but very much alive, and his familiar eyes are a warm brown.

As the Boy King approaches AUDRINNE, CAM pulls the pen from his pocket.

RAIK: You have no right to ask me anything. But perhaps grief has driven you mad. So in deference to your tragic loss, I will tell you to your face: go back to Aquitan.

AUDRINNE steps back, confused, and the crowd murmurs.

AUDRINNE: What loss?

RAIK: Your wife was killed last week when rebel forces overran your house.

AUDRINNE: My . . . wife?

RAIK: Perhaps you should have brought her to the ship as my decree suggested. But you can still save your son. Get to the *Prix de Guerre*. Those of you who stay will regret it soon enough.

His face red, his eyes lost, AUDRINNE turns to LEGARDE.

AUDRINNE: What do you plan to do about this?

LEGARDE: I plan to get the living to the ship.

AUDRINNE sags, all bluster gone, and turns back to RAIK.

AUDRINNE: Are you sure she's dead?

CAMREON: He's sure.

The pen hidden by his hand, the Tiger steps lightly up the stairs, approaching the Boy King.

Le Trépas likely told him. Didn't he, Raik?

RAIK only stares at CAM, his eyes wide. The crowd rumbles, uncertain, but AUDRINNE lashes out.

AUDRINNE: Who the hell are you?

CAMREON: I'm Camreon Alendra. The rightful king. And I'm sorry to say that Le Trépas killed your wife, like he killed my brother.

Suddenly CAMREON lunges, grabbing RAIK by the arm. It takes just a moment to make the mark—death—but the Boy King doesn't fall. Instead, he rips the pen from CAMREON's hand as the crowd gasps. RAIK looks down at the mark on his hand, then up at his brother.

RAIK: You've always thought I was a puppet king. These are my only strings now.

Pulling aside the neck of his robe, he reveals the puckered scar on his throat, surrounded by the healed marks of ugly stitching. CAMREON's mouth opens—closes. For the first time in a long time, the Tiger looks lost.

CAMREON: You were dead.

RAIK: You only wished I was. Guards!

The shout jolts CAMREON into action. He bounds down the stairs and plunges into the crowd as the palace door swings open again and more Aquitan soldiers pour through the door.

Bring me the Tiger. Show the rest of them to the docks.

As the soldiers swarm toward the crowd, the Aquitans at the front recoil, while those in the back push closer to see what's going on. Those in the middle cry out in the crush. But AUDRINNE is not ready to give up.

AUDRINNE: Aquitan soldiers obey the Aquitan general!

LEGARDE: You heard him. Bring them all to the docks.

Furious, AUDRINNE raises his gun. LEGARDE's hand darts out to grab his wrist. AUDRINNE gasps as his bones creak in the general's grip.

I've given you a lawful order. For your safety, and your son's, I suggest you obey.

He pushes AUDRINNE back toward his carriage, and the man stumbles down the stairs. The soldiers follow him, fanning out before the palace steps to push the Aquitans back. On the other side of the plaza, CHEEKY yelps as someone grabs her hand, but it's only AKRA.

AKRA: Time to go.

LEO: Thank the gods you're here. Get her back safely, will you?

Before AKRA can reply, LEO disappears into the swirling crowd toward the palace—toward LEGARDE.

CHEEKY: Leo! Come back!

She cannot follow; AKRA holds her tightly. But at the sound of CHEEKY's shout, RAIK's head turns.

RAIK: Cheeky?

Their eyes meet over the heads of the crowd. Then the king points, calling to his armée.

The Chakran girl! Bring her to me unharmed!

The soldiers turn to look at her, and finally CHEEKY lets AKRA pull her away. The crowd flees with them, trying to escape the plaza. As they careen toward the side street,

*they meet another line of soldiers standing side by side in
a blockade.*

*The men are nervous—never before have they faced
their own people. But they are here on the general's orders,
and so they press forward, funneling the Aquitans toward
the sea.*

*AKRA doesn't stop, and the crowd parts around him,
repelled by his uniform. When they reach the cordon, a young
soldat stands in their way. He glances nervously at CHEEKY,
then back at AKRA.*

SOLDAT: Orders are to bring everyone to the docks.
*AKRA lifts his chin with all the condescending authority he
developed when he was a real capitaine.*
AKRA: She's Chakran, not Aquitan.
*The young soldat narrows his eyes, unsure, but finally he
nods, stepping back. Then, over the crowd, RAIK shouts.*
RAIK: There she is! Don't let her go!

*The soldat jumps at the king's orders. Then he draws his gun
with shaking hands. Before he can point it at CHEEKY, AKRA
grabs the weapon, jerking it sideways as the soldier fires. At
the sound of the shot, the crowd screams. AKRA grunts at the*

pain of the bullet. Then he punches the soldier once, twice, thrice, until the man reels away.

Blood streaming down his side, AKRA pushes CHEEKY toward the safety of the alley. Behind them, the crush has turned into a riot. Men in the crowd have drawn their guns on the soldiers, and the soldiers shoot back. Slowly, the "Chakratans" are herded to the docks, LEO along with them.

CHAPTER

TWELVE

Theodora and I follow the servant through the glittering maze of the palais, passing massive friezes, marble statues, fine porcelain, and framed paintings. The endless carpet underfoot is soft as fur, though it's been woven with such intricate care that it feels like a shame to step on it.

Beside me, Theodora seems unaffected by the grandeur; her brow is furrowed and her eyes faraway. "A ship for a shadow play," she murmurs, speaking in Chakran. "Can you do it?"

"How big a ship?" I try to laugh, but I had heard the stories of Le Roi Fou's generosity. How he had given a favored shadow player her weight in gold, or offered his own throne for kindling when a fire ran too low for a third encore. Like all my dreams of Aquitan, my trust in those tales has faded. But walking through the fine halls, with my dirty feet on the priceless carpet, they seem a lot more real. "They say your uncle is mad for fantouches, but I didn't realize how bad his malheur really is."

"Shh." Theodora flicks her eyes toward the servant, then back. "Don't assume he doesn't know what he's doing."

"What's he doing, then?"

"I'm not sure," she admits. "It might have something to do with public opinion of the occupation. The last thing my uncle needs is a rebellion on his own soil, and spending more money on a failed war looks different than spending money on popular art."

"What about spending money to save Aquitan lives?" It is difficult for me to keep my voice to a whisper. "How can he believe Le Trépas is harmless?"

"Could he afford to believe otherwise?" Theodora's own face is troubled. "If Aquitan knew the monk's true abilities, no one would ever have come to live or work in Chakrana. Not to mention fight," she adds. "Safer to paint Chakrans as victims of their own superstitions. After all, you have to admit, harnessing souls sounds . . ."

"Crazy?" I say with a bitter smile, but she shrugs a shoulder.

"Improbable."

"You believed," I say.

"I grew up in Chakrana," she counters. "And I saw what you did with the first avion. Remember, I'd been trying for weeks to get that machine airborne. I knew it was something more than science. It's probably for the best my uncle is skeptical," she adds with a familiar gleam in her eye. "Or he might be more protective over the Keeper's book."

"Le Roi said the book was blank," I remind her.

"And I can't see the souls in this hallway," she replies. "That doesn't mean they aren't there for someone who knows how to look."

Automatically, my eyes flick across the little lights drifting in the air. She's right, of course, but before I can tell her so, I realize that the servant ahead is watching us with the blank expression servants here seem to cultivate. He stands beside a door carved with leafy patterns reminiscent of bromeliads, opening it with a flourish as we approach. "Your rooms. There are refreshments laid out on the buffet, and chemises on the beds."

Theodora thanks him, but any reply I might have made

flies out of my head when I step inside. The Chakran suites, the king had said, though it is less Chakran than the idea of Chakrana.

Silk in bold colors has replaced the ubiquitous velvet on the Aquitan-style couches, and orchids in full bloom are displayed atop the marble mantel of a grand fireplace— at home, fire is only made for cooking or shadow plays. The plasterwork continues the leafy motifs, as do the gilt frames of the art on the walls. There are fantouches here, finely wrought and lovingly painted, but each one is pressed useless—lifeless—under glass. The paintings themselves feature Chakran scenes as well, though with that strangeness that comes from the distance between knowledge and imagination. In one, villagers work in pastoral sugar fields, where the sun is mild, the humidity low, and the serrated leaves of the cane never meet bare skin. In another, half-dressed girls splash in a jungle pool, completely unconcerned about mosquitoes.

It is a uniquely Aquitan understanding of Chakrana— all surface, no substance. No soul. If anything, the room is even more foreign than the rest of the palace.

At least the food looks delicious. There is an entire tray of those little flaky pastries on the table, along with more fruit and cheese, and something unidentifiable that smells like meat but resembles paste. As I reach for a tiny pie, I see a silver flask beside the platter. Picking it up, I uncork the bottle. The contents look like water, but I know better.

"The elixir," I say, weighing the flask in my hand—so heavy. Not even the promise of a ship seems as extravagant. "There's enough for weeks in here. Maybe months!"

Theodora only smiles as I tip a dose into the cap and drink it down. "We should get some rest," she says, taking a handful of fruit and turning toward a bedroom. "It's been a long day."

"Good night," I say as she closes the door softly behind her. The thought of bed is tempting. Then again, so are the pastries. I stand over the table and eat three in rapid succession. Then I pick up a fourth and find my own room.

The spacious chamber has yet another fireplace to ward off the chill in the air, and the bed is a mountain of pillows and blankets, framed with carved mahogany posts thicker than roof poles. Luxurious curtains of gold velvet hang in swags—much heavier than the mosquito nets I'm used to, though there are no mosquitoes here.

There is a long white nightgown laid across the foot of it, clean and soft as morning mist, but suddenly I am too tired to undo the buttons on my borrowed dress. Instead, I fall face-first into the feather bed, still clutching the flask of elixir. But when I close my eyes, I can see the gleam of the monk's dark smile.

Thankfully, sleep comes for me quickly, and it seems only a moment before golden light pries my eyes open again. Struggling out of the mound of bedding, I squint at the bright sun through the glass windows; now I understand the purpose of the heavy velvet curtains lining the bed.

I had dreamed of lights—not the morning sunlight or the gleam of souls, but the flicker of flames at my back, and dark shadows dancing on the scrim. Though I hadn't seen him in my dream, I'm fairly sure the king was in the audience. My brother had been there too, hadn't he? I lie in bed, trying to remember what show we had been performing, when his voice comes again, knocking the shreds of the dream out of my head. "Jetta?"

"Akra?" I sit up, bleary-eyed, and he snorts.

"Are you still sleeping? It's mid-afternoon!"

"Really?" I glance back through the window. Outside, the sun is at a gentle angle in the sky. "I think it's still morning here."

"Here?" I can hear the puzzlement in his voice. "Where are you, exactly?"

I hesitate. "In Aquitan."

"Aquitan? I thought you were going to get the elixir!"

"I did . . ." Frowning, I paw through the pillows until I find the flask again. It is still warm from my hands. "I have it. But the Keeper's Book of Knowledge is here too, and it may help us stop Le Trépas."

"Cam mentioned that," Akra says slowly. "But he didn't say anything about the two of you going after it now."

"It was a last-minute decision," I say.

"It often is, with you. But it's probably for the best you're so far away."

"Why?" He doesn't answer immediately, and I'm suddenly very awake. "How are things in Nokhor Khat?"

"There's good news and bad news," Akra says cautiously.

"Good news first."

"Well," he says slowly. "I'm pretty sure we're all still alive."

"That's the good news?" My mouth goes dry. "What's the bad news?"

"Raik is still alive too," Akra replies. "Your blood didn't work on him."

I clutch the flask tighter. "So . . . he wasn't dead when Cam found him during the battle at the temple?"

My brother sighs. "It was dark. There was a fight raging outside. And the scar looks fairly bad," he adds. I can imagine the bitter smile on his own scarred face. "It would have been an easy mistake to make."

"But . . ." I shake my head—it makes no sense. "Why would Raik work with Le Trépas willingly?"

"We didn't exactly get a chance to ask him," Akra says. "But my guess is for the power he can offer."

"Power?" An uneasy feeling bubbles up in my stomach— Le Trépas had offered me the same thing. "But Raik is a king."

"He knows Camreon belongs on the throne," my brother says with a scoff. "We all know. And there are two ways someone can react when their sibling is more powerful than they are: pride, or envy."

The uneasiness grows, but I try to laugh it off. "Are you proud of me then, Akra?"

"I was just about to ask you the same question," he replies, and I laugh again, for real this time. But he doesn't laugh along. "That isn't all the bad news."

My smile falls away as quickly as it came. I look once

more to the window, facing east. The city hides the sea, which in turn hides my country. My family. My friends. "What is it, Akra?"

"Leo went after Xavier. We're going to bring him back," he adds quickly, but I'm still trying to make sense of the words. "I almost didn't tell you, but—"

"What do you mean, bring him back?" My heart is pounding. "Where is he?"

"He's at the dock with the rest of the Aquitans," Akra says. "But the *Prix de Guerre* doesn't leave for two days yet."

"The *Prix de Guerre*?" My stomach flips—deportation would be the least of Leo's worries. "What if Xavier kills him—or Le Trépas finds him first?"

"Believe me, I wish he'd thought of that before running off," my brother replies, but I'm already scrambling out of bed. Forget the Book of Knowledge, forget the ship. I already have the elixir. I need to wake Theodora and get back to Chakrana.

"I'll be there by tonight," I say, wrenching the door open. Then I freeze at the sight of a Chakran woman in the sitting room.

For a moment, I am certain it's Maman—but how could she have gotten here, to Aquitan? And although this woman is about the same age, she is plumper—well fed—and much more comfortable in an Aquitan gown than Maman would ever be.

The woman stares back at me, a cautious look on her face. Then her eyes flick to the empty room behind me. Had she heard me talking—shouting? I shut the door again quickly as my brother's voice echoes in my head. "No," Akra says firmly. "Stay where you are. I don't want to have to worry about you running off too."

"Akra—"

"You need to find that book," he says. "Le Trépas might not have raised the Boy King, but he's still the one in control. Stopping him is the best way to end all of this."

"Yes, but—"

"Know your role, Jetta. And let me play mine."

I grit my teeth—it's something he always says. But my role isn't to sit by while Leo is in danger. Still, it's no use arguing with my brother about it. "If you don't want me to give you orders, you should give me the same courtesy," I hiss, but his only response is silence, and I know in an instant that I've gone too far.

My fingers curl around the neck of the flask—of course his orders to me are different from mine to him. He had told me once how it felt: the pressure like a hand around his heart, the sensation of the air being pressed from his lungs if he did not leap to obey. It is the last thing I should threaten him with. But before I can form an apology, a knock at the door makes me jump. The Chakran woman's tentative voice drifts into the room. "Mei mei?" Younger sister. When was the last time Akra called me that?

"Just a minute," I call back through the door, but my brother's presence is already fading from my head. "Akra?"

There is no answer. With a sigh, I rest my forehead against the gilded panels. I'll have to apologize in person. But no matter—I'll be there soon enough.

Gathering my composure, I pull the door open. The Chakran woman is standing just outside. "Pardon the intrusion," she says, and now I can tell what reminded me so much of Maman. It is her poise. Her posture is impeccable, her hands folded neatly in front of her, and she wears a friendly smile like an accessory. This is a woman used to being watched. "Court is abuzz with news of the latest shadow player," she continues. "And possibly the last. I had hoped to introduce myself and hear some news from home."

The word—home—is rich in her mouth, and looking at

her in her Aquitan gown, I can imagine how much it might mean to her to sit and talk about Chakrana. But I need to get home myself. "I'm sorry, jie jie," I say—older sister—and her eyes crinkle as her smile broadens. "But Theodora must be waiting."

"You mean Mademoiselle La Fleur?" The woman turns, glancing across the sitting room to the open door of Theodora's bedroom. "I heard that the king summoned her early this morning."

"She didn't wait for me?" I cross the sitting room, peering into Theodora's bedroom, but the room is empty, the bed already made. I frown, glancing out the window once more. Perhaps it is later than it seems. Or maybe Theodora was only eager to see the book.

I return to the sitting room, unmoored. Suddenly I realize I do not know how to deal with the king without her help. Am I expected to wait for my own summons, or can I go to him myself? But I can't let local customs stand in my way. "I should go find them," I say, with more certainty than I feel.

The woman's smile freezes. "Dressed like that?"

I falter on my way to the door, looking down at my gown. It was bad enough last night, travel stained and oversized, but now, rumpled from sleep, it's even worse. "I don't have many options," I say, trying to smooth out the wrinkles. "I had to pack lightly aboard the avion."

"Very lightly," she murmurs. "I heard you need to borrow fantouches for your upcoming performance."

I frown, trying to tame my tangled hair with my fingers. "Is there nothing the court doesn't gossip about?"

"Any shadow player knows that the only thing worse than an audience is no audience at all," she says wryly, and the claim brings me up short.

"You're a shadow player?" I say, but of course she is. I had been too distracted to recognize it before.

The woman only smiles, reaching out to take my hand. At first, I think she means to shake it, Aquitan style, but instead, she turns my palm up, placing her own beside it. "I always look at hands," she says softly. White scars shine on her own skin, so similar to mine, though she must have gotten all of hers by working with leather—making fantouches. "Art always leaves its mark. I'm Ayla," she says then, releasing me. "Of the Ros Sook."

"The Ros Sook!" My eyes widen, I can't help but bow. The troupe had been famous when I was a girl, but I hadn't heard of them in years. Of course—they'd won recognition at the Fêtes des Ombres and went off to Aquitan, never to return. "It's an honor to meet you," I say at last. "I'm Jetta of the Ros Nai."

"The honor is mine," she says warmly. "I've never heard of a one-woman troupe."

"I usually perform with my family," I tell her, trying to ignore the pang in my heart. "But they're still in Chakrana."

"Ah," she says, her expression turning sympathetic, her eyes lost in memory. "When my own troupe first traveled to Aquitan, it took me years to save enough to bring the rest of my family here. It seems much harder to do it all alone. If you ever need help, I'd be happy to give it."

"Thank you, jie jie," I say—the offer is a kind one, and if I were to stay, if I had more time, I would love to take her up on it. What stories could she tell? "But I plan to return to Chakrana as soon as the show is over."

"What?" Her face is a cascade of emotions—shock, worry, confusion. "Why?"

I stare at her, taken aback. It is one thing to hear such a question from the king, but quite another to hear it from a Chakran. "Chakrana is my home," I say—hadn't she just said the same?

The look she gives me reminds me once more of

Maman, so much it makes my heart ache. "A home is hard to defend, with war and hunger knocking at the door. Not to mention Le Trépas," she adds with a shudder. "He's on the loose once again, I hear."

My face falls; my back stiffens. Guilt floods in. "Le Trépas will be stopped," I say firmly. "The war will end, and Chakrana will be stronger than ever."

"But how long will that take?" She shakes her head sadly, and anger pushes the guilt aside. I glance pointedly at her Aquitan dress.

"It would certainly be faster if our best hadn't fled to Aquitan."

Ayla only raises an eyebrow. "Do you think no one suffered in Chakrana before the Aquitans came? There are rich and poor in every country. The real enemy is want," she adds, but Le Trépas's words echo in my head. Know your enemy. "Here in Aquitan, you can defeat it."

"That's wonderful for the Aquitans," I say. "What about the Chakrans who can't leave?"

"You and I are artists," she says. "Not fighters. Not saviors."

"Why not all three?" I say. Know yourself.

"If you want to excel, you must choose . . . especially

here." The advice is not so strange, but the look on her face is. As though she is afraid—not of me, but for me.

"Why?" I ask, narrowing my eyes. "What's so different about Aquitan?"

She wrings her hands, her knuckles pale and taut. Where is her poise now? "There have been artists who tried to fight," she says at last. "To bring politics into the theater. But Le Roi doesn't only reward the people who please him. He will punish the ones who don't."

Despite the fire in the hearth, a chill goes through me. But before I can ask what punishment she means, a firm knock echoes through the room. Without waiting for an answer, a servant opens the door, and behind him, I catch sight of a gaggle of courtiers in the hall.

For a moment, I fear Le Roi had somehow heard us talking about him, and that the courtiers have come to see me arrested, or worse. But the servant bows so low that his lips nearly brush his knee. "Mademoiselle Chantray," he murmurs to the carpet. "Le Roi requests your company."

The request itself is a mere formality—the servant is barely done speaking when the king himself breezes through the door. Though his smile is warm and bright, it does nothing to dispel the cold feeling in my chest. But

Ayla's poise has returned; she bows, and I do the same, smoothing my features into a smile. "Your Majesty."

"Good morning, Jetta," Le Roi says, inclining his head to us both. "And Ayla. I shouldn't be surprised to see you here. Ayla makes a habit of welcoming all newcomers from Chakrana."

"I appreciate the visit," I say softly. "It's always good to know more about my audience."

"After all these years, she is still one of my most prized players," the king says fondly. "You would do well to learn from her."

Ayla's smile deepens at the praise—just so—and she presses a hand to her heart, moving so deliberately that she might as well have been a puppet herself. "Thank you, Your Majesty."

"Speaking of shadow plays," the king says, turning back to me. "It is time to choose your fantouches. Allow me to show you the Salon des Merveilles."

Outside, the courtiers echo his words in a susurration of whispers. I am reluctant to leave, but when I turn back to Ayla, her smile hasn't budged. "A pleasure," I say. "I hope we meet again."

"So do I," she says, but despite the pleasant look on her

face, the words feel ominous. As I hurry to the king's side, the crowd parts around us, and Ayla's whispered warning seems to follow.

I wish Theodora was here. I am ill at ease in the king's company, especially without her. I glance back over my shoulder, but she is nowhere to be seen among the following courtiers. "Is La Fleur waiting for us in the salon?"

"Alas," the king says. "My dear niece is . . . otherwise occupied."

The tone of his voice gives me pause, but I can't imagine a single thing that would keep Theodora from the Book of Knowledge. "With what?"

"Her health, I'm afraid." The king shakes his head sadly. "I have long heard stories of the madness brought about by the jungle, but I had hoped Theodora's strong mind would resist it."

"Madness?" I stare at the king, sure for a moment I am misunderstanding his Aquitan. "Theodora?"

"You heard her last night, talking about dark forces and evil influences. And of course, her request for the elixir," he adds with a pointed look. The marble floor seems to shift beneath my feet. The flask is heavy in my own pocket; I'm sure the king had heard her say it was for me. But the courtiers hadn't—they'd only known a bottle was being sent to our rooms. The king sighs heavily, loud enough for them to hear. "But don't worry. At Les Chanceux, she has the best docteurs, and excellent care."

"She's at the springs?" I say, my heart racing. "When will she be back?"

"Not the springs," the king says, stopping briefly before a wide doorway. The servants rush ahead to open it, and late-morning light spills through. Outside, a carriage waits in the square, and the king glides blithely toward it. "I had a sanatorium built there years ago," he says over his shoulder as I rush to catch up. "Sanatorium—do you know the word? Less educated people might call it a madhouse."

ACT 2,
SCENE 13

Back at the Royal Opera House. TIA and ELLISIA sit cross-legged on the stage, playing a card game. There is a small stack of Aquitan bills between them, as well as a much larger stack in front of Ellisia.

ELLISIA: I win again.

She puts down her cards with a flourish and adds the smaller stack of money to her own.

I'd say we should play double or nothing, but we're already there.

TIA: It was your money in the first place.

ELLISIA laughs, handing the entire stack of bills back to TIA.

ELLISIA: Aquitan money. It's worth as much as you paid for it, these days. At least winning it back passes the time.

TIA: I'm definitely grateful for that.

Chewing her lip, TIA glances at the door, the way she has two dozen times over the last few hours. With a sigh, she takes the deck of cards to reshuffle. She is dealing when she hears the creak of the stage door. Cards scatter as she springs to her feet.

Oh, thank the gods. There are only so many times I can lose at cards.

CAMREON and CHEEKY slip inside the theater, followed by AKRA. He shuts the door behind them, leaning heavily against it, his hand over the wound at his side. CHEEKY sinks down into the nearest velvet chair, drawing her knees up and wrapping her arms around them. But TIA looks at the door, then back to CHEEKY.

TIA: Where's Leo?

AKRA: He's caught up in the cordon with the rest of the Aquitans.

TIA: You left him behind?

CAMREON: He wasn't supposed to be there in the first place!

CAMREON stalks down the aisle as CHEEKY glares at his back.

CHEEKY: He needed to find Xavier.

AKRA: We found him, all right.

AKRA pushes off the door, wincing, then follows CAMREON to the stage.

Can I borrow your knife? I have to get this bullet out.

CAMREON hands over the blade, and AKRA climbs the steps toward the stage. CHEEKY's expression shifts from frustration to worry.

CHEEKY: Do you need help?

AKRA: I can take care of it. There's a needle and thread in the costume shop.

He vanishes into the shadows in the wings. Meanwhile, CAMREON starts to pace. TIA glances from him to CHEEKY, wide-eyed.

TIA: What happened out there?

CAMREON: My brother isn't dead.

ELLISIA: You sound surprised.

CAMREON grits his teeth.

CAMREON: I thought he'd been brought back to life by Le Trépas. But it turns out he's in the grip of something worse.

TIA: What?

CAMREON: Jealousy.

He sits on his heels, running a hand over his face.

ELLISIA: Well, I could have told you that.

Looking up, CAMREON glares.

CAMREON: I'm all ears.

ELLISIA: What about my concert?

CHEEKY stands, incensed.

CHEEKY: They have Leo! Anything you know could help us get him back!

ELLISIA: My livelihood is made selling what I have. Leo would respect that. So should you.

TIA: What about collateral, then?

She reaches for the violin case, but CHEEKY snatches it away, glaring at ELLISIA.

Cheeky.

CHEEKY holds the violin close for another moment, but ELLISIA raises an eyebrow.

ELLISIA: You're Cheeky? Raik has plenty to say about you, as well.

CHEEKY wavers, then looks at CAM.

CHEEKY: You better be ready with the treasury the minute you're on that throne.

At his nod, CHEEKY slides the violin case across the floor, and ELLISIA stops it with her hand. Then she sighs, patting the leather of the case.

ELLISIA: In all honesty, I don't think Raik realized what life was like outside of Nokhor Khat—or even outside the palace. Before he left to join the rebellion, he was so sure of himself. But when he saw the rest of his country—the work and the sacrifice of everyday life—he felt out of place. Then, of course, you both betrayed him.

CHEEKY: I never—

ELLISIA: His words, not mine. You were the girl he couldn't have.

She gestures at CAMREON.

And you were the leader he couldn't be. But if he can't be loved, Le Trépas can make him feared.

CAMREON: He told you all of this?

ELLISIA: There are lots of ways to make someone feel good. Listening is one of them.

CAMREON: I see.

The Tiger folds his arms, frowning at ELLISIA as he considers his next move.

How often does Raik send for you?

ELLISIA: Almost every night—like I said, he's a long-standing client. Not that I always come when called.

TIA snorts.

The inn keeps me busier than I'd like, and to be honest, the palace is . . . not what it was.

CAMREON: How so?

ELLISIA: The servants are gone. The whole place is empty. And it stinks. Most of the time I send some of my girls to take care of business. Before you ask, we're not going to poison him for you. Even if you could afford it. I won't take the risk.

CAMREON: I wasn't going to ask. I don't want him dead.

From the shadows backstage, AKRA reappears, his wound bandaged. There is a bitter smile on his face.

AKRA: Because he's your brother?

CAMREON: Because I should have known.

He sits on his heels, rubbing his forehead.

I thought he just needed time to adjust. That seeing life outside the capital would help him be a better king.

TIA: Maybe he didn't want to be a better king.

CHEEKY: I don't think he wanted to be a king at all.

She chews her lip as she turns to CAMREON.

When you left him in charge of the rebels, he was more worried about how to get champagne shipped to the jungle than about how to get the armée out of Nokhor Khat.

AKRA only shakes his head, looking at CAMREON.

AKRA: The Tiger would kill him for aligning himself with Le Trépas.

CAMREON: I'm not the Tiger anymore, remember? I'm the rightful king. What will Chakrana see in me if I start my reign with my brother's blood on my hands?

ELLISIA: They'll see Le Trépas, and La Victoire, when your own parents were killed.

CAMREON swallows. The memory is a very old wound, but that only makes the pain more surprising.

CAMREON: Yes.

AKRA: Do you really think you can convince him to

step aside? Let you take over?

The Tiger hesitates, sharing a look with CHEEKY.

CAMREON: It depends on who asks.

AKRA's mocking smile falls away.

AKRA: Not Cheeky.

CHEEKY: Yes Cheeky. He said he wanted me alive.

AKRA: So he could kill you himself.

CHEEKY: Not if I play my cards right. What are we offering?

CAMREON: A life of luxury, funded by the treasury. No responsibilities. And you.

CHEEKY: Also funded by the treasury, I presume.

AKRA: Cheeky!

At his cry, she turns to him, but the anguish on his face gives her pause; it is much worse than the pain he'd shown over the bullet. She goes to him, gathering his bloody hands in her own.

CHEEKY: Akra . . . it's just a job. My livelihood, like Ellisia said—

AKRA: I know. But I'm . . .

He hesitates, glancing at the others, then lowering his voice to a whisper.

Afraid.

CHEEKY: So you can face danger, but I can't?

AKRA: Yes, exactly.

CHEEKY laughs, but TIA comes to her side, reassuring.

TIA: I'll go with her and keep her safe.

AKRA: I thought you were a lover, not a fighter.

TIA: It's wartime. There's rationing. We all have to make do.

CAMREON: I'm coming too.

AKRA: After your performance on the palace steps? I doubt you'll get past the door.

CAMREON: I'll be in disguise.

AKRA: They're bound to check for weapons.

CAMREON: Anything can be a weapon, if I need one. You heard Tia. We'll make do.

Outnumbered, AKRA turns back to CHEEKY.

AKRA: Even if they can keep you safe, I'm supposed to just let you go?

CHEEKY: I won't be gone long. Raik only wants me because I rejected him. If I come crawling back, he'll be bored of me in a couple of weeks.

AKRA: What if he isn't?

CHEEKY: Well. If all else fails, *I* don't have a problem poisoning him. Ellisia—can you help us get into the palace? I'm sure Raik would pay extra for the girl he couldn't have.

ELLISIA considers as she turns to CAMREON.

ELLISIA: And you plan to lift the deportation decree?

CAMREON: I do. In fact, I plan to send Akra to stop the *Prix de Guerre* from leaving the harbor.

ELLISIA: It's a deal. I wasn't made to be an innkeeper.

AKRA spreads his bloody hands in a disbelieving gesture.

AKRA: Am I supposed to stop the ship by myself?

CAMREON: You're the best suited for it. After all, Le Trépas can't steal your soul. And I'll order the dragon to obey you. Can you do it?

AKRA narrows his eyes, then turns back to CHEEKY.

AKRA: Depends on who's asking.

CHEEKY: Please, Akra.

She leans into him, her head against his chest.

Leo is on that ship.

AKRA wraps his arms around her tightly—fiercely.

AKRA: If you swear you're coming back to me as soon as you can.

CHEEKY: Of course I'm coming back.

She pulls back, giving him a pointed look.

Cam's not the only one who owes me.

AKRA: What do I owe you?

CHEEKY: This.

She rises up on her tiptoes to kiss him, and he holds her for a long time before he lets go.

CHAPTER
FOURTEEN

The madhouse.

I feel it in my throat—a rising heat, like fire, like bile—a scream, building with my rage. Looking into the king's guileless eyes, I would bet my life that he knows Theodora doesn't belong there.

Was this a punishment, like Ayla said? The king had been displeased by his dear niece's attempt at public humiliation, and he is in full control of the audience as we cross the plaza to the carriage. The courtiers are following, watching, whispering. Not to mention the guards at the door, and the footman approaching to help me up the step. Le Roi Fou has staged all of this with impeccable timing. Moreover, he knows I'm the one who really needed the elixir. If I protest too much, too loudly, it would be only too easy for him to whisk me away to the sanatorium as well.

Swallowing my anger, I take a breath, searching for the right lines on this impromptu stage. "This is shocking news," I say slowly as the footman offers me his hand. I take it reluctantly—in the carriage, I lose the audience. "Theodora Legarde is the sanest person I know."

"She's been under incredible strain," the king replies. "The loss of her father . . . the embarrassment of her brother. But time heals many wounds."

"Surely a visitor would help," I say over my shoulder as I step into the carriage. "I'm one of her closest friends."

"Perhaps once the worst is over," the king replies smoothly as I settle into the velvet seat. "Unfortunately, her delusions center around Chakran superstitions. I'm not sure she'd be well served by seeing someone who shares them."

His voice rings over the square—only when he is finished does he follow me into the carriage, leaving the whispering courtiers behind. I grit my teeth as the carriage starts across the cobbled square.

Nécromancy is far from superstition. I want to prove

it—to raise a fantouche here and now. To tuck the soul of a butterfly into his silk handkerchief, or the spirit of a frog into one of his shoes. But looking at Le Roi Fou's hawklike face, I remember when I had tried to impress his half-brother with my power. Maman had explained it all away with lies: hidden strings, a trick of the light. If I am to prove myself to the king, I need something unmistakable—inexplicable except by the truth.

Then again, do I want him to know the extent of my powers? My hand goes again to the little scar in the crook of my elbow, where the armée stole my blood and then used it against me—against my country. I have to be very careful when facing the king. And I have to do it without Theodora's help.

My mind is spinning faster than the carriage wheels, the way it always does under strain. Can the king tell? Does his own malheur do the same?

"In happier news, the court is very much looking forward to your performance," he says. "The theater is ready as soon as you are, and I have a very capable orchestra to place at your disposal."

"An orchestra," I say, and I no longer want to scream, but laugh. Half a year ago, I was ready to leave Chakrana for this chance. But now the same price seems much too high. And yet . . . an idea begins to form. Know your role, Akra had told me. If I need to convince the king of anything, where better to do so than on a stage? "And fantouches, you said?"

"In the salon," the king says, gesturing out the window. "Here we are."

The carriage rolls to a stop, and when the footman opens the door, I see we haven't gone far. Stepping down from the carriage, the great cathedral of Lephare looms over me, the soullight brighter than the morning sun.

Up close, the building itself is even more impressive: taller than the kapok trees that rise above the rest of the jungle, and carved as richly as our own temples are—or at least, as they were. Grotesque creatures and lovely faces peer from the corners and the lintels, though I don't recognize the stories they must represent. Even stranger: the arched doors of the church are flung open, and people drift in and out as freely as the souls. Is this how our temples had been—how they could be again?

But when the king descends from the carriage, he starts along the side of the building, away from the main doors. "Where are we going, Your Majesty?"

"The Salon des Merveilles is beneath the cathedral," he

says again, lifting a hand. The footman races to his side, holding out an embroidered kerchief. The king puts the perfumed fabric to his nose, and even I can smell the spicy scent it carries—cinnamon and sandalwood. But on the wind, there is a more familiar smell. Death. "The entrance is unfortunately close to the churchyards," Le Roi adds, his voice muffled through the cloth. "The smell is usually much reduced in the cooler of autumn weather, but we wanted the work completed before the ground freezes, and so quite a few of the graves are open."

As we approach, I understand his meaning. At the edge of the plaza, behind a low stone wall mottled with moss and lichen, a small armée of men turns the muddy soil. With their shovels and their carts, they could almost be farmers, but their harvest is bitter: piles and piles of pale bones, plucked from the earth and stacked neatly into the backs of the carts.

The sight wakes a memory: my brother and me, playing in the jungle beyond the fields and paddies. We'd been gathering sticks and vines to build a stage for shadow plays when I'd pulled a dirty leg bone from the leaf mold. Akra and some of the other village children went hunting for the skull, but the first one he found was much too small to belong to the same body as the femur. We ended up finding half a dozen skulls before it started to get dark; most of them had holes in the backs, and one even had a brass armée bullet rattling inside.

We had told our parents, but what could they do? Our makeshift stage in the jungle was not the only place where bodies had fallen. I watch as the men sift vertebrae from the churchyard muck—Chakran men, I realize, and men from the Lion Lands. Their features are obscured by the cloths tied around their mouths and noses, but I can see the rich shades of their skin.

Why am I surprised? Chakran shadow players weren't the only foreigners who came to Aquitan—anyone could, if they were brave enough to leave and could save enough to buy a ticket. But in my country, foreigners got the best jobs. Here, it seems most of us are offered the worst. Except for the lucky few: the artists, like me. Like Ayla. But only as long as we didn't displease the king.

As I watch the men working, one of them stands, pressing his filthy hands to the small of his back. Hurriedly, I look down, so he doesn't catch me staring— so he doesn't see my face, or recognize my features. I'm ashamed to be walking into the treasury at the king's side, instead of standing in the muck with my own people.

Le Roi continues to the back of the cathedral, where a pair of guards stands by a plain wooden door. They wear ceremonial swords on one side and more utilitarian guns on the other, but they step aside when they see us approaching. Le Roi pushes the door open without needing a key, and cold air rushes out of the spiraling stone stairwell.

The footman races ahead, lighting the lamps on the way down, but the souls are even brighter than the flame. They cluster so thickly here beneath the cathedral, spiraling through the air, racing up and down the steps, flickering like embers in the corners. I don't realize I am staring until the king calls back over his shoulder. "Is something wrong?"

"No," I say quickly, hurrying to catch up. "I'm only surprised to see a treasury beneath a temple."

"The jewel room and the gold vault are in the palace itself." The king's voice echoes up the stairwell. "But Le Trépas is not the only dignitary who has honored me with strange gifts. We need a place to store them."

"Strange gifts?" As the stairs spill us out into a stone room the size of a warehouse, I can see what he means. Wooden shelves line the walls all the way to the vaulted ceilings, and each one is covered in valuables—from stringed instruments, to blown-glass vases, to architectural models, to an enormous boat carved of a single knotted trunk. When I catch sight of a beast lurking in the corner, my heart leaps into my throat before I realize it's stuffed. The creature is three times as large as a water buffalo, with armored plates instead of fur and a single horn sprouting from the wide nose.

"The people of the Lion Lands call it a rhinoceros," the king says when he sees me staring. Then he points to the ceiling, where the articulated bones of another creature hang: a strange amalgamation of animals, with great wings and an eagle's beak, but four paws like a cat. "And they claim those are the bones of a griffin, though I'm fairly certain it's only spare parts, strung together by a charlatan. Speaking of which, there is the book Le Trépas brought," he adds, nodding.

"Ah." The implication is a needle in my side, but this is not the time or place to argue with Le Roi about power and trickery. Instead, I follow his gaze to the dusty shelf. I had expected a thick tome, but the Book of Knowledge is surprisingly slim.

Before I can pick it up to look inside, Le Roi beckons me farther into the salon. "These will be more interesting to you," he says.

Reluctantly, I tear my eyes from the book, but when I come to his side, the sight takes my breath away. The shelves on the far wall are covered in fantouches, and each one is a marvel: gorgeously painted, richly dyed, finely tooled and scraped, gilded and studded with sparkling gems. Thoughts of the book fly out of my head, and my fingers reach out, almost involuntarily. "There must be hundreds," I whisper.

"Thousands," Le Roi corrects me, and I can't summon a reply. How much work did this collection represent? To see them gathering dust on the shelves makes my heart ache. I run my hand over the fantouche of a tiger. The stripes are like flames, and gold rivets articulate at least twelve joints in the tail. There is another beneath it—a dragon with ruby eyes, each scale dyed a slightly different shade of shimmering red. Out of the corner of my eye, I see Le Roi smile. "I was hoping you might perform as soon as tomorrow."

"Tomorrow?" I turn to him, my mouth dry. Even with an orchestra at my disposal and a thousand fantouches to choose from, it is soon—too soon. I'd need at least a week to truly impress the court; I don't even know which show to perform. I am about to tell him so when I remember that I never meant to stay. "Tomorrow," I say again, returning to my study of the fantouches. "Yes. But I need some time to look through your collection." I need time to read the book as well.

"Bien." The king goes to the stairs, where the footman waits. "I myself need to visit the engineers' corps to check progress on the avion. I'll come back this afternoon to show you the theater."

I am admiring another fantouche—the elegant coils of a sinuous serpent—and the words take a moment to hit my ear. I frown. "The . . . avion?"

"Yes," the king says over his shoulder. "The one you arrived in, so dramatically. I've set my engineers to disassembling it."

"Our avion?" I drop the fantouche to stare at the king, but he only cocks his head.

"*My* avion," he corrects me. "My own engineers built them, all to Theodora's specifications. Strangely, we were never able to get them aloft. But Theodora did," he says, his eyes glittering in the light of the souls. "Since she's too indisposed to tell me how, I've asked my engineers to figure it out."

I stare at the king, wide-eyed. Now I know why he has put her under guard in the sanatorium—she would not explain how the avions functioned. I had seen the king's letter to Theodora, the one that had urged her to come home. He had long trusted—even coveted—her knowledge. Her genius. Now he's found a way to claim it for himself.

The accusation is on my lips, but it is likely only because Theodora hasn't told him the truth that I am not a prisoner myself. Here in the vault, with no audience but the footman, I have little doubt that could change in a moment. Quickly, I smooth my expression, reaching for calm—I have always been a good actor. "How am I expected to get back to Chakrana, Your Majesty?"

"Chakrana?" Le Roi chuckles a little, as though disbelieving. "I still can't understand why you'd want to go back. But remember, I promised you a ship in exchange for a show." He sweeps up the stairs, the footman following. "Best make it good."

ACT 2,
SCENE 15

Night has fallen at the docks in Nokhor Khat. The Aquitan refugees are clustered along the water's edge as the armée guards the side streets. Those nearest the cordon argue and plead with the soldiers, but their response is by rote: the general is coming, take it up with him.

BERTRAND AUDRINNE has retreated into his carriage with his son. He has lit the lamp that hangs on the side of the carriage; his son has always been afraid of the dark. LEO, on the other hand, uses nightfall to his advantage. He has picked up an Aquitan hat, tilting the brim down to obscure his features as he searches for his brother. He had lost sight of XAVIER in the scrum, but the soldiers seem sure he's on the way.

On the west side of the docks, the refugees stir as the cordon opens for a cart pulled by a skittish water buffalo. Bodies are stacked in the back—those who had been trampled or shot in the riot. The crowd draws back quickly as the Chakran driver steers toward the pier; not even in death are Aquitans allowed to remain in Chakrana. Behind the wagon marches a line of stone-faced soldiers. The general leads them, and when the crowd sees XAVIER LEGARDE, they rush back, clutching at the sleeves of his uniform. They call to him, demanding help, action, salvation, but the general only raises a hand in a gesture meant to be calming as he continues toward the ship. His soldiers follow in silence, looking straight ahead.

LEO hears the general's name long before he sees him over the heads of the crowd. Reaching AUDRINNE's carriage, he clambers up on the back wheel, trying to find a path forward. Better to head to the Prix de Guerre than to try to fight his way through the knot of people clustered around his brother— or rather, his brother's body.

LEO's hand goes to the gold necklace he wears under his shirt: the circular symbol of the Aquitan god. His brother had worn it until the day he'd died. His other hand goes to his breast pocket, where the pen holding Jetta's blood is tucked away. Then he jumps at the sound of AUDRINNE's voice.

AUDRINNE: What are you doing, boy?
LEO: Désolée, monsieur—
AUDRINNE: Get off my carriage or I'll shoot!

AUDRINNE fumbles at his waistcoat, but LEO drops back quickly into the crowd.

LEO: I would save my bullets if I were you.

LEO picks his way toward the pier, reaching the ship just as the wagon arrives. The soldiers start to unload the bodies, carrying them up the gangplank while the general steps onto the wagon seat beside the Chakran driver.

Immediately, the Aquitans fall quiet. The general looks out over the crowd, sympathy in his eyes. LEO, in the front of the crowd, pulls his hat lower so the general won't recognize him, though part of him hopes his brother could.

LEGARDE: My fellow Aquitans. I regret it's come to this. But perhaps it was foolish to think our fight in Chakrana would ever end peacefully. Regardless, it is over. Our future lies across the sea. It's time to go home.

The crowd stirs at the speech—it isn't much, but they are desperate to hold on to something. And hearing the words in his brother's voice brings tears to LEO's eyes. If he hadn't been there . . . hadn't watched him die . . . hadn't held the gun himself . . . LEO might not think twice about the fact

that the general's speech to the Aquitans was given entirely in
Chakran.

As his soldiers take the last body from the wagon, the
general beckons to the crowd.

LEGARDE: Come, then. Let us leave with dignity and
arrive in Aquitan in order. Leave your weapons and any
luggage here on the docks. My men will stow each item
safely. Le Roi Fou has asked me personally to take note of
any valuables you had to abandon in your homes. He plans
to make full restitution upon your arrival.

The crowd stirs again, this time more hopefully. As the
general steps down from the wagon, a line of Aquitans
follows. Not all are so easily convinced, but the cordon
of soldiers still block the side streets, and the line is only
growing.

LEO himself has snuck in third, and he waits patiently
as the two men before him detail their plantations, their
wealth, their riches left behind. By the looks of their suits,
the descriptions are only wishful thinking—then again, so
is the promise of restitution.

As the second man finally moves up the gangplank, LEO

steps forward, the pen clutched in his hand, but the general puts his own hand up.

LEGARDE: Stop.

LEO freezes, sweat rolling down his face under the brim of his hat. He glances at the water, gauging his distance to the edge of the pier. But the general only jerks his chin toward the wagon bed where the men before him have left their pistols.

LEGARDE: Surrender your gun.

LEO wets his lips, but the question comes out like a croak.

LEO: Why?

LEGARDE: Safety. Quarters will be cramped, and tensions high. We don't want a repeat of what happened at the plaza. Don't worry. My men and I will keep the peace.

With his free hand, LEO pulls out his gun and tosses it into the cart. The general beckons him forward, turning to the booklet in his hand.

LEGARDE: Name?

LEO braces himself.

LEO: Leo—Leonin.

There is no recognition in the general's eyes as he writes the names, as though they're first and last.

LEGARDE: Leo Leonin. And what have you had to leave behind?

LEO's shoulders fall.

LEO: My brother. Xavier Legarde.

Now the general looks up, surprised, but LEO is ready. His hand darts out, making the mark of death on the back of the general's hand. He cannot see the soul that springs out—or the way it flees, as though afraid—but his brother's body falls in a heap on the pier.

    A cry goes up from the crowd, but LEO doesn't stop to watch the panic spread. Spinning on his heel, he bolts for the water, but before he can dive in, a strong hand pulls him back. Not the soldiers—but the Chakran driver of the cart. The man smiles at LEO from under the broad brim of his own wide hat.

    LEO has found LE TRÉPAS.

LE TRÉPAS: You know there are crocodiles in the water.

LEO struggles to break free, but the soldiers have reached him by now. As they haul him to his feet, LE TRÉPAS plucks the pen out of LEO's hand and smiles.

Bring him aboard!

To LEO's surprise, the soldiers obey.

LEO: What are you doing? Don't listen to him! That's Le Trépas!

Ignoring his cries, the soldiers drag him up the gangplank. Desperate, LEO headbutts one of them hard enough that he hears the crunch of the soldier's nose. The man only grunts as blood seeps from the break in sluggish brown clots—LEO recoils as he realizes these soldiers are already dead.

On the dock, the terrified crowd surges away from the general's body, from Le Trépas, from the Prix de Guerre. *But in the streets behind the cordon, more uniformed men appear, and these have been dead much longer.*

Their skin sags in the humid heat, their eyes are sunken in their sockets. Some have bloodstains on their uniforms, or crusted around their ears. The bodies are clearly weeks old—likely from the battle at the temple— but with the general fallen, LE TRÉPAS has given up on pretense.

Guns crack and men scream as the dead soldiers push even the living armée toward the ship. Underneath the noise, the word is like a melody: nécromancy. Now the

Aquitans fall back, fleeing from the dead men, and the ship is the only place to go. Scrambling up the gangplank, some Aquitans lose their footing, tumbling into the water as crocodiles approach.

On the dock, a gunshot rings out—then another. Desperate to escape, AUDRINNE has clambered up to his own carriage seat, firing not at the soldiers, but into the crowd.

AUDRINNE: Make way! Make way, damn you!

His horses stamp and snort as he tries to turn his carriage around, but one of his compatriots returns fire. AUDRINNE clutches at his chest as a red wound blooms on his uniform. In the carriage, his son begins to cry.

Taking the reins in bloody hands, AUDRINNE snaps them as hard as he can. Smelling death, the horses need no more encouragement; they careen across the dock, not toward the cordon of revenants blocking the city, but toward the blackened sea.

In the dark, they don't even hesitate at the edge of the pier. The splash throws water onto the dock, and the horses panic as the carriage fills with water, pulling them

*inexorably down. As the lamp winks out, the boy inside
pounds on the window, but the door is locked. AUDRINNE
closes his eyes, leaning back against the driver's seat as the
water surges over his son's head and the epaulets of his old
uniform.*

CHAPTER
SIXTEEN

The king's footsteps fade up the stairs, followed by the distant drum of the heavy door as he shuts me into the salon with the rest of his marvels.

I count another five heartbeats, to make sure he's far enough away. Only then do I scream, the sound shaking the souls of bats from their perches on the vaulted ceiling.

Le Roi Fou has taken Theodora, he has taken our avion. For practical purposes, he has taken my freedom, offering it back in exchange for a show. Not that I could leave without Theodora, even if I did have a ship. And how long would a journey by ship take? A week at least. What would happen to the *Prix de Guerre*—and to Leo?

Rage burns in my belly—was the elixir really worth this? I rip the flask from my pocket and heave it across the room. It crashes into the shelf, denting the old wood and tumbling into the fantouches with the unmistakable tinkle of breaking glass.

The sound jolts me, turning anger into fear. Despite the dust coating the embarrassment of riches in the room, I have a feeling Le Roi Fou would know instantly if something were destroyed. What had I broken? I go to the shelf to retrieve my flask. There is something dark on the corner—I try to brush it away, but it smears on my fingers like ink.

Cursing, I shove the elixir into my pocket, then scrub my hand on the inside hem of my dress. Pulling out the rest of the fantouches, I check for stains. The tiger I'd seen earlier is still pristine, as is the dragon beneath it. I set it aside on the carpet, then pull out a fantouche of the King of Death, and a second dragon, even more impressive than the first.

I am relieved when I find not so much as a stray spot on any of them. But the fantouche at the back of the shelf is not so lucky. The limbs clack gently as I lift it out. It is not fashioned out of leather, but wood, painted brightly and inlaid with chipped gems and nacre. This puppet is not for shadow plays—it's meant to be seen without a scrim. It's cleverly made, with a head that spins to show different faces: an old man, a beautiful youth, a fierce warrior, a young girl. With a start, I realize it's the Keeper, made to perform the story of the Keeper and the Liar—the same story I'd seen carved on the stairs at the temple. The ink had come from a tiny glass bottle hanging from a string beneath the puppet.

The bottle is smashed now. Such a fragile thing: the gift of a deity. Still—there are a dozen plays about the Keeper. Unless you knew the puppet was made to tell that particular story, you might not notice the bottle of ink was missing. Taking my little knife, I cut away the string holding the bottle, setting the broken glass carefully on the shelf. Once the ink dries, I'll slip it into my pocket and dispose of it outside.

Gently, I return the fantouche to its place at the back of the shelf. The nacre eyes shine in the shadows there. The Keeper's look is accusing. What am I doing? I had come here for the book, not to destroy the king's fantouches, and certainly not to have a temper tantrum in the bowels of the old cathedral. Akra was right; I have a role to play. But I don't know my lines—or even what performance I am meant to give.

Save Theodora. Save Leo. Bring back the elixir, bring back the book. A ship for a show, the Mad King says, impressing me with the treasury, threatening me with the sanatorium.

My thoughts are racing again. Was that the king's goal? Was he trying to keep me off balance, to destabilize me? I can't let it happen. I take a deep breath, the way I do before any show, when my mind starts burning like the flames in the fire bowl and the lines threaten to trip over each other on their way past my tongue. If I am to play my role, I have to do it one beat at a time. So what first—what now?

The Book of Knowledge, of course. Theodora wouldn't have it any other way.

It is nestled between a gilded glass vase and a scrimshaw tusk. Seeing it here, surrounded by so much glittering treasure, I can see why the king thought so little of it. The book is much plainer than I expected, bound in undyed leather, with no gilt or title. But if it is the Keeper's book, it might just be the most valuable thing in the room. After all, knowledge is power, isn't it? Or so the stories go.

Reverently, I pick it up. A thin layer of dust swirls away, glittering with the souls of dust mites. I have worked with leather all my life, making fantouches, but I have never seen a grain so fine. Is this really the body of a deity? Suddenly, my hands are trembling.

I sit cross-legged on one of the soft carpets covering the stone floor, setting the book on my lap so as not to drop it. But when I turn to the first page, it is blank, just as the king had said.

Determined, I flip through, looking carefully for anything—a sign, a symbol, a mark—but there is nothing, not even on the covers. Were we mistaken to think this was anything more than an empty book? Perhaps it was foolish to believe that Le Trépas would give the king a holy relic— but why would he give the king a book at all?

Maybe there was a secret to it . . . a way to reveal the writing. Le Trépas must have known it, or guessed. His powers and mine take blood to summon. Wouldn't the Keeper's work the same way?

With my little knife, I prick my fingertip and mark the book on the first page—not with the symbol of life, but the symbol of knowledge. To my surprise, the blood soaks into the page, then vanishes.

Nothing else happens.

But the symbol usually has an accent, doesn't it? Know yourself, know your enemy—my thoughts are racing again.

I take another deep breath, but my hand shakes as I press the knife against my palm. The air hisses out through my teeth; the cut is deeper this time. But as the blood wells up, I use it to write both symbols.

Nothing.

I try "life" instead, then "death," but the symbols only sink into the paper and fade the same way. Frustrated, I shut the book and toss it on the carpet beside me. But why would my blood work? I should be trying the blood of someone who serves the Keeper—like the monk at the temple at Kwai Goo. But even if her blood would have illuminated the writing, she is dead, and we burned her body. I wrinkle my nose as the acrid smell of burning hair returns—a memory, a hallucination. Trying to focus, I shut my eyes and pinch the bridge of my nose, but now all I can smell is the iron tang of blood.

My own power comes through my lineage—the blood Le Trépas and I share. But he killed all of my siblings. Was the blood gone for good? Death begets life, he had told me once. What begets knowledge?

Perhaps the Keeper's monks would know, if we could find them. If we could bring the book back to Chakrana. If we could get back ourselves.

The monk's taunting smile swims in the dark behind my eyelids. Frustrated, I open my eyes, staring at my hands, bloody, scarred, and stained with ink.

The ink . . . the Keeper's gift.

Slowly I turn back to the book on the carpet. Could it be that simple?

My hands shake as I pick up the broken bottle, trying desperately not to spill the last drops. I dip my fingertip into the remaining ink and open the book, marking the first blank page with the Keeper's symbol: knowledge. Just as the blood did, the ink sinks down and disappears. But this time, it floats back up, swirling like a black storm on the page, and settling into new words:

What would you like to know?

THE KEEPER
AND THE LIAR
Part 2

In the days when our ancestors were young, stories began to fill the world, but the Keeper still did not know how the first story ended.

So the Keeper watched and waited until they found the soul of the liar in her next life. She was still full of stories, but now she had no time to tell them.

Instead, she woke at dawn to care for her youngest daughter, and stayed up late with her eldest son. And as the sun crossed the sky, she tended to her parents, and her husband, and their humble house and their tiny farm, and she cleaned the soot from the fire after cooking meals and wiped the sweat from her brow after washing clothes. When she fell into bed at night, she was too tired to tell stories, even in her dreams, for work of the mind is a luxury to those who work so hard with their hands.

But art and truth have their own power, even over the gods, and so the Keeper came to the liar's door, and when she opened it, they gave her three gifts.

The first gift was ink, mixed from the soot of her fire and the sweat of her brow.

The second was a secret that only the Keeper knew, about a rich man with no heirs who had buried his wealth under a tree.

The third was a shovel.

CHAPTER SEVENTEEN

In the Room of Wonders, with the Book of Knowledge open on my lap, I stare at the Keeper's question on the page. How exactly does one speak to a deity? Though I have prayed at times, this is much different: never before had I expected an answer.

Would they tell me anything? Everything? But what did I want to know? What had Le Trépas asked—and did I want the answer?

"Is Le Trépas really immortal?"

I am out of ink, so I speak the question aloud, hoping the Keeper can hear me. Seconds pass like hours as I wait.

Then the ink seeps back into the page, rising up in new words. "He is."

"How?"

"Forbidden magic." The answer comes in dark swathes of ink. "Stolen blood."

My hand goes to the scar at the crook of my arm. "Mine?"

"This was long before you were born," the Keeper replies. "The blood came from the last servant of the Maiden. One of your previous incarnations," they add, and my heart flips in my chest. "It is good to see your soul again."

I reread the words twice before they fade. More questions bubble up in my own mind. I had wondered, as we all have wondered, what other lives our souls have led, though speculation had become an Aquitan parlor game: Madame Audrinne herself had been half convinced she'd lived a past life as a famed princess. I have a feeling that the Keeper would tell me my own distant past if I asked, but do I want to know how that girl lived? I can guess how she died. "Le Trépas killed her."

"Only her heart's blood could cast a spell that would outlive her."

I shiver, and not from the chill air in the Salon des Merveilles. "What spell was it, then?"

"Life, death, and knowledge." The symbols sweep across the page, lighter now. "With her blood, and mine, and his, Le Trépas drew his own soul from his body and put it somewhere else for safekeeping. The magic is forbidden for a reason," the Keeper adds quickly, as though worried I will try it. "He is something less than human."

"I don't want to use the spell." My lip curls at the thought. "I just want to know how to kill him."

"A man without a soul cannot be killed," the Keeper replies. "You must find where his soul is hidden, and return it to his body."

"Where is his soul?"

"I don't know."

I blink at the page. "You're the Keeper of Knowledge," I remind them.

"I keep knowledge that souls give me." The words grow fainter still; I can barely read them. Lifting the book, I tilt it toward the light. "I have not seen Le Trépas's soul in a long time. And unless you free it from wherever he put it, I won't for ages yet."

"Do you have any clues?" I say, my desperation growing. The soul could be hidden in anything, anywhere. "Anyone who saw him do the spell?"

"There aren't many souls who can reach me here, on a dusty shelf in Aquitan," the Keeper replies, but the last words fade into nothingness.

"What if I bring you back to Chakrana?" No reply comes. I pick up the broken pot of ink and scrape at the bottom with my fingernail, but the dregs flake away like dried blood. Sitting back on my heels, I stare at the blank page. Now I know why Le Trépas left the book in Aquitan. Not only to hide the deity from the rest of us, but to hide knowledge from the deity themself. The armée needed entire battalions to disassemble the temples and erase the old ways, but Le Trépas had silenced a god with his own two hands.

The hypocrisy enrages me, but as much as I want him dead, the monk's soul might have to wait. If I can bring the Keeper back to Chakrana, they may gather more information as souls come their way. Of course I have to convince Le Roi to let me keep the book first.

Did I have anything left to bargain with? Anything I would be willing to give up? But the king had already taken everything he could. What if I were to offer a second show? An encore performance? The thought is daunting: how long would I have to stay in Aquitan to earn a ship and the book as well?

Then again, if I could find another way home, I could tell Le Roi the ship was unnecessary. But how? How? My thoughts are racing again, leaping from topic to topic like a spark in a room full of kindling. Frustrated, I flop back onto the pile of fantouches, trying to breath, to focus. Overhead, the souls flit along the vaulted ceiling and through the hollow bones of the griffin. Such a strange creature, part cat . . . part bird.

As I stare at the broad wings, laughter bubbles up from my belly until it echoes to the stone arches. Of course I have a way home—I only have to climb up to take it. I cast about for something to stand on, but even the tallest chair in the room is not enough. But why use a chair at all?

I had heard another story once—a foreign story, from the Lion Lands—about a green silk carpet dyed with magic to make it fly. I don't have dye, but I do have blood, so I coax down one of the souls of the bats clustered along the ceiling and draw it into the rug beneath me. It wobbles and flutters as it rises, but it's steady enough to bring me safely alongside the pale bones of the enormous beast. When I make the symbol of life on its back, I make sure to pull a bird's soul inside.

As she settles into the body, the bones creak and groan. Then the whole skeleton twists, swinging wildly on the thin ropes that hold it to the ceiling. If the beast flexed its wings, I'm certain the strings would snap. For a moment, my mind is aflame with the image: bursting into the light on the back of the griffin, with the book in one hand and the elixir in my pocket, leaving the king to curse the empty sky behind me.

The thought delights me—the joy and the power in it. It is only with great difficulty I push the image from my head. That may be the final act, but there is one more beat to play. Theodora is still at Les Chanceux, locked away in the sanatorium, and Le Roi will not release her as long as he thinks she can give him the secret to flight.

Of course, that secret is not his to take. I need to show him that. No . . . not only him. I need to show all the Aquitans. Theodora had the right idea the night we'd arrived, when she'd made the avion circle above the palais until the audience had grown. The king relies on public opinion—the rebellion in Chakrana is proof of that. And I will have an audience, won't I? At the Royal Opera House tomorrow night.

Gently, I stroke the bony spine of the griffin. "Be patient," I whisper, and she stills just as I hear the heavy scrape of the door opening above.

Has the king returned already? Frantically, I push the

carpet back to the floor as his footsteps echo down the winding stairs. Squeezing the last bit of blood from my palm, I yank the bat's soul out of the silk threads. Then I straighten up, my heart pounding, my cheeks flushed, but the carpet is flat on the floor, and the bat's golden soul hangs off the motionless skeleton of the griffin.

"Good afternoon," Le Roi calls as he reaches the bottom of the stair. Then he narrows his eyes. Can he see how flustered I am? "Have you chosen what show you'll perform?"

"Of course," I say, almost before the answer comes to me. The Keeper and the Liar is the obvious choice. A reliable standby—every troupe has a version—and though I'm sure the king has seen it before, I can make it new again. But my thoughts keep churning as I follow Le Roi's eager gaze to the fantouches still scattered on the floor. The King of Death is there, holding his lamp, beside the tiger, with its long tail draped gracefully across the stone.

The Keeper and the Liar is about truth in art. The king needs to know the truth about power. A new idea flickers across my mind's eye, painted on a scrim in shades of black and gold, dark and light. Then I jump when the king speaks: his question seems to echo off the stone walls. "What show will it be?"

"The Shepherd and the Tiger." As the words tumble out, they seem so right, but the king's eyebrows go up.

"I thought I knew all of the old stories," he says. "But I must admit, I've never heard that one."

"It's the show we'd meant to perform at the Fêtes des Ombres," I say. "Adapted from the story of the swineherd."

"Ahh." The curiosity on the king's face shades into recognition—and something more. Reminiscence. "My late brother was sometimes called the Shepherd of Chakrana."

"He was the inspiration," I say, remembering the man who called himself a shepherd, despite the fact that my country had no sheep. I hadn't understood it back then—the way the general had looked at us as though we were mindless animals in need of protecting. But I have seen it in the king's eyes, in the way he dismisses both our fears and our power as mere superstition.

Still, I know enough to keep my thoughts out of my own expression, and the king's smile deepens. "I look forward to the performance," he says. Then he gestures to the pile of fantouches at my feet. "I'll have the servants gather these up and bring them to the opera house. Let me show you the space, so you can prepare."

"One more thing, Your Majesty," I say, feeling bold. Is

it my malheur, or only that I finally know my role? The king turns back, a waiting audience. "I've been thinking about the ship you promised," I tell him. "I'm not sure I'll need it."

"But how will you return to Chakrana?" he asks, his words an echo of my own. Is he trying to mock me? His expression is innocent, but I know better. Never underestimate him, Theodora had said. Know your enemy.

"You were right," I say, dropping my eyes so he can't see the truth in them. "There is much more for me here than there ever was in Chakrana."

"Indeed," the king agrees. Rage flares in my chest; I turn away quickly to cover.

"Can I make another admission?" I say, picking up the book with a gesture I hope looks casual. "In return for my performance, I'd much rather have this."

"A blank book?" In the light of the souls, the king's eyes seem to glitter. "Why?"

I wet my lips, my mouth suddenly dry, but the truth gives me my lines. "There is a legend in my country," I say, my voice low enough he has to hold his breath to listen. "About a priceless relic, kept safe in a temple for centuries. One day, Le Trépas stole it and brought it to Aquitan. A

Book of Knowledge," I add, offering it to the king. "Said to hold all the secrets of the dead."

The king cocks his head, then glances down at the book. There is a strange look on his face, almost hesitant, as he takes it from me. As though here, under the earth, surrounded by the dead he cannot see, he himself feels the pull of what he calls superstition. Does his hand tremble as he opens the book? But when he sees the blank page, he throws his head back and laughs.

"The knowledge of the dead! Of course," he says, still chuckling. "Very amusing. I can imagine your own disappointment."

"The book taught me a valuable lesson," I counter, with a small smile—just so. "I would like to keep it as a reminder of all the things I leave behind me."

"Bien," the king says, closing the book and tossing it carelessly back on the shelf. "It's all yours after the show, though I think you're a bigger fool than I am not to ask for something else! Now come," he adds, wiping tears of laughter from the corners of his eyes. "Let's go see the opera house."

ACT 2,

SCENE 18

Night in Nokhor Khat. Flowering vines hang in bowers over the path, and night moths flit through the perfumed air. On the narrow path, ELLISIA leads CHEEKY, TIA, and CAM to the garden gate of the Ruby Palace. Surreptitiously, CHEEKY adjusts her dress.

ELLISIA: Are you uncomfortable in the dress, or uncomfortable with the plan?

CHEEKY: The plan is fine.

She plucks at the waist of her lavender gown, then looks sidelong at CAM.

I should have chosen the green sarong.

ELLISIA: Raik prefers a more Aquitan style. Besides, the green is better on Camreon.

CAMREON makes a face as CHEEKY adjusts her dress again.

CAMREON: Thanks.

TIA nudges him with a gentle smile.

TIA: Are you all right?

CAMREON: You tell me.

He gives her a bitter smile.

It was . . . difficult to look at myself in the mirror.

TIA: You look—

CAMREON: Don't say "beautiful."

TIA: I would never. But you are well disguised.

CAMREON: I suppose that's something.

ELLISIA: We can still go back.

She hesitates, looking at CHEEKY particularly.

We can all still go back.

CHEEKY: With all the money you stand to make?

ELLISIA: I'm a madame, not a monster. I'll wipe the books if you want to turn around.

The look on ELLISIA's face is genuine, but CHEEKY is resolute.

CHEEKY: No. We can do this.

Raising her chin, she smooths her gown one more time, then folds her hands demurely and continues on to the palace.

Outside the entrance, two Chakran men stand guard—both apparently alive. Not so the dog chained between them. The slavering creature stands as ELLISIA leads CAM, CHEEKY, and TIA to the gate. The guard on the right, TAMAR, narrows his eyes.

TAMAR: Four of you?

TIA: Variety is the spice of life, they say.

ELLISIA: Only three tonight, Tamar. I have business at the inn, but the ladies can keep Raik good company. Especially Cheeky.

ELLISIA nods at the showgirl.

I heard Raik has been looking for her.

TAMAR stares as the other soldier reaches for CHEEKY's arm. ELLISIA slaps his hand away.

Look with your eyes, Soro!

SORO rubs his hand, off balance, looking to TAMAR.

TAMAR: I don't think the king will be interested in the others.

ELLISIA: I don't think you know him like I do.

She gives the guard an arch look, but he doesn't move. The easy smile falls from her face.

They come as a set or not at all. Unless you want to get the king out of bed to tell me otherwise.

SORO still hesitates, but TAMAR waves them forward at last.

TAMAR: Come on then.

CAMREON hesitates, looking at the dog.

CAMREON: Does he bite?

TAMAR: Not if you're unarmed.

TAMAR eyes the rebels with a slow grin.

You're not hiding anything under those gowns, are you?

CAMREON musters his best smile, which is more like a grimace, but TIA winks, stepping forward.

TIA: Down, boy.

Her saucy smile barely falters when the dog stalks closer, but the soldier was right. The beast only sniffs wetly at her hands, then sits back down on sagging haunches. TAMAR gives them a mocking bow as SORO opens the gate.

TAMAR: Welcome to the palace.

CHAPTER NINETEEN

When I was a girl, I had dreamed of seeing the Royal Opera House of Lephare, but as the carriage rolls through the streets, I am afraid to watch for it out the window. Like all things in Aquitan, I fear it will disappoint me . . . betray me. That the reality cannot compete with my childhood imagination—or even worse, that the king's smugness will spoil my awe. But when I catch sight of the theater out the window, those worries vanish.

It is a grand building, taking up an entire city block, and the front is lined with rows of columns topped with gilded arches. Tucked into each alcove are tall marble figures holding musical instruments. It looks like a temple dedicated to some god of the arts, though in the fading light of the afternoon, the marquee is lit with gas lamps, not soullight.

I have seen the imitation in Nokhor Khat, but this version is grander somehow—taller, I think. Or is it only that here, in Lephare, the style of the building is less out of place?

As we pull up by the wide steps, I don't bother waiting for the footman to help me out of the carriage. Le Roi climbs down at a much more stately pace, and we walk side by side up the wide steps. The footman hurries ahead to open one of the many arched doorways; at the end of a performance, every door would be flung open to the evening air, the audience spilling excitedly down the steps with music still echoing in their ears. I can almost hear it myself—the strains of a song—as we enter the lobby.

Stepping into the opera house is like walking into a jewel box. Overhead, deep coffers frame painted scenes that decorate the ceiling. The detailed walls shine gold in the light of a thousand candles. The gas lamps make them unnecessary; the chandeliers are only for show. Had the servants lit them all just for the king's visit? But even after such a display, stepping into the theater itself takes my breath away.

A sea of seats in gold and red sweeps down toward a massive stage, framed in columns so high they look like they're holding up the ceiling. Between them hangs a silken scrim big enough to shelter the entire population of my old village in sudden rain. It is woven as a single sheet of fabric, so no seams would mar the view of the performance. Above my head, tier after tier of balcony seats rise like the layers of a fanciful cake, and along the walls, gilded boxes lean toward the stage to get a better view.

"What do you think?" Le Roi asks. I search his face, knowing he can see the answer on my own. Does he only want me to say it aloud so he can gloat? But it would be foolish to deny the truth.

"It's . . . beautiful." The song in my imagination is louder here, echoing in my ears, with low drums like Maman used to play. I hold my breath, concentrating, and Papa's voice joins the drumming: a Chakran song, here in the heart of Lephare. But I'm the only one who can hear it—at least, for now. "I wish my family could see it too."

"I give my best players a pension. Many of them have used their pay to bring their relatives from Chakrana." The king shrugs, as though the custom is a strange one, but I am well acquainted with it. "If you're as good as you say you are, you can earn much more than an old book."

"I am the best," I murmur as shadows flicker in the corner of my eye. Not the story of the Shepherd and the Tiger, but one I haven't yet told.

In it, a family steps from a pier onto a boat. The shadow of the vessel cuts a trim line across the swirling blue waves of the wild sea, until a gleaming city rises out of the water: Lephare. I can see the skyline in my head, oddly familiar by now—the spire of the great cathedral, and the lines of the grand palais. The song in my head swells, followed by a storm of applause.

What would my life have been like had the rebels not attacked at the Fêtes des Ombres?

When the king speaks, his voice makes me jump. "Tomorrow night, I will see for myself."

"Tomorrow," I repeat, chewing my lip, but as the word sinks in, the echoes of applause fade. Suddenly I am filled with dread. The stage is the biggest I've ever seen, and there are thousands of seats to fill—thousands of people to cheer my success, or to jeer at my failure.

"The maestro should be by shortly to discuss your

choice of music," the king adds. "Ah! And here are your fantouches."

From the lobby, a line of servants appears, silk bags slung over their backs. Horror grows in my chest as they deposit the bags at the foot of the stage: I can't even remember which fantouches are inside. The King of Death, the tiger . . . but was there anything I could use for a shepherd or sheep? Peeking into one of the bags, I see the scales of a stray dragon. Panic wraps cold fingers around my throat. There is no dragon in the story of the Shepherd and the Tiger.

Where is the confidence I felt in the Salon des Merveilles? The grand visions, the certainty of success? It has all vanished like a charlatan's trick—and my malheur is behind it.

The king is unaware of my mounting reservations as he breezes up the aisle. "I'll leave my footman in the lobby, in case you need anything else for the show," he calls over his shoulder.

Should I hurry after him? Tell him I'd made a mistake, that I need to return to the Salon? No—bad enough I have lost my own confidence. If I lose his now, I might never get it back.

Instead I turn to the stage, but now the music in my head has vanished, along with the visions of the shadows on the scrim. Where are the ideas that had bubbled over one another in the salon? My mind is blank, like the pages of the Keeper's book.

With difficulty, I try to summon the story in my head. "In the days when our ancestors were young," I murmur, trying to recall the song, but without Maman's music, the rhythm is elusive. "There was a brave swineherd who tended well to his . . . No. There was a brave *shepherd*." The words sound wrong in my voice: Papa had always been the one to sing the stories. Still, I should know the new words—I was the one who had written them! But that show had been meant to flatter a man I had later killed. . . . Is that why it escapes me now?

I had been a different person then. I hadn't known what I know now. I cannot tell that story.

So what story can I tell?

I don't want to flatter Le Roi. I want to tell him the truth about power, and the truth is that he has never tended well to anyone but himself.

But even if I told that story, would he listen? Ayla's words come back to me—other shadow players have tried before. Then again, other shadow players didn't have all the skills I do.

Standing in the audience before the grandest stage I have ever seen, a new idea sparks in my head. A show like no one has ever seen, including me. But for this performance, I will need different fantouches.

I'll need help too, and I know who to ask. Returning to the lobby, I send the footman for pen and paper. When he returns, I dismiss him with my thanks, citing the need for privacy to focus. Only when the door shuts behind him do I start my letter. Words, so elusive before, seem to spill onto the page. When I finish, I fold the note so it has wings like a bird, and sign it—not with ink, but a drop of blood.

"Find Ayla of the Ros Sook," I say to the soul that creeps inside, and I watch the letter flutter up to the gilded ceiling and wheel away into the night.

Fighter . . . artist . . . savior. I told you this morning that I cannot choose, and so I cannot stay in Aquitan. Before I go, I will put on a show the likes of which no one has ever seen, for I am not only a fighter, or an artist, or a savior. I am also a nécromancien. But although I have the dead to help me, I need your help as well. Please meet me at the opera house as soon as you can.

ACT 2,
SCENE 20

In the stateroom of the Prix de Guerre. *LEO struggles on the fine wool carpet, tied hand and foot. He has managed to wriggle his way toward the stern, where a broken latch protrudes below the sill. Working desperately, he saws the rope against the rough edge of the metal, working until his shoulders ache and his wrists are numb. But at last the rope loosens, and he shrugs off the bindings to start untying the ones on his ankles.*

Just as he manages to free himself, the cabin door begins to creak open. Hurriedly, LEO shoves his hands behind his back and tucks his feet beneath him, as though he is still bound.

LE TRÉPAS enters the room, carrying a birdcage in one hand and a stained burlap sack in the other. A frightened bird sings from the cage, but LEO's eyes are fixed on the bag: from the rounded shape and the rust-red stain spreading on the burlap, it is not rice inside.

Setting the birdcage down on the deck, the monk turns back to LEO, a smile on his face.

LE TRÉPAS: Where is Jetta?

When LEO doesn't respond, LE TRÉPAS lifts the bag.

Perhaps you'll answer if your brother asks?

LEO: Xavier's soul is long gone.

LE TRÉPAS: All I need is a drop of blood to bring it back.

LEO turns his face away.

LEO: If you're so all-powerful, what do you need Jetta for?

LE TRÉPAS: Isn't it obvious?

LE TRÉPAS throws the bag down at LEO's feet, where it bounces with a dull thud, landing near his knees. LEO shrinks back.

The dead rot. A living armée is much more reliable.

LEO: She'd die before giving you an armée.

LE TRÉPAS: But will she let you die?

LEO growls, but the monk only goes to the desk, rummaging in the drawers until he finds a piece of paper and a pen—this one full of ink.

LEO: Why do you need an armée? You've gotten what you wanted. The Aquitans are leaving Chakrana!

LE TRÉPAS looks up from his writing, raising an eyebrow in surprise.

LE TRÉPAS: Do you really think I'd go through all this trouble just to send a few hundred Aquitans home? Better to teach the rest of them never to come back. Now if you'll excuse me, I have a letter to send.

Tossing the pen to the desk, he pulls out the other one, the one full of Jetta's blood, and marks the letter with the symbol of life. Of course, nothing happens—souls flee Le Trépas. The monk only turns to the birdcage, opening the door to reach inside. As he wraps his fist around the feathered body, the bird flaps frantically, then stops.

LEO looks away, but soon enough, the fluttering sound returns, this time from paper wings. The monk follows the note to the window at the stern, watching it fly away—not inland, but across the water.

LE TRÉPAS: She's in Aquitan?
LEO looks up, startled.
LEO: She is?
LE TRÉPAS: Why? Why did she go there?
For the first time, the monk looks troubled—almost frightened. He rushes toward LEO, wrapping his bloody fingers around LEO's wrist.
LEO: She was looking for her elixir! That's all I know!
The monk narrows his eyes, but LEO's face—and his fear—

are genuine. LE TRÉPAS releases the boy's wrist.

LE TRÉPAS: No matter. We're going there anyway. But if she can't give me a living armée before I arrive, I might as well get started on a dead one.

The monk turns on his heel, heading to the door, but LEO calls after him, trying to keep the panic out of his voice.

LEO: You're going to kill the Aquitans? Now?

LE TRÉPAS: It's a lot of flesh. A lot of blood. Best to start early.

LEO: You said it yourself, the dead will rot before we're halfway to Lephare!

LE TRÉPAS: Not with Jetta's blood powering the ship. I have just enough left to take one more soul. What do you think? A crocodile, perhaps? They'll be easy to catch.

As LE TRÉPAS heads toward the door, he picks up the rice sack that holds XAVIER's head.

Especially with a little bait.

As the monk exits, LEO spares a last look for the open window at the stern.

LEO: One more soul.

Gritting his teeth, he sheds the last of the rope and stands, racing after the monk.

ACT 3

The Swineherd
and the Tiger

In the days when our ancestors were young, there was a brave swineherd who tended well to his charges. Under his care, his herd grew numerous and healthy, and the swineherd happy and prosperous.

Then one day, a tiger came prowling. The beast was quick and deadly, carrying off livestock night after night. The other farmers locked their doors, too frightened to face the tiger, but the swineherd guarded his herd closely, so the tiger stayed away.

After three nights, the swineherd was exhausted. He fell asleep during his watch and woke to the cries of the smallest runt being carried away in the jaws of the tiger.

Quickly he gave chase, with only his staff to defend himself, while his neighbors called after him to let the tiger go. But the swineherd knew that if he let the tiger go now, the beast would only come back. So he chased the creature through the fields, across the valley, up the hills, and into the jungle, where the King of Death was waiting to collect a soul.

There the tiger dropped the piglet and turned to face the swineherd, a hungry look in his eye. "You could have let me go with just a morsel," the tiger said. "Now I have a feast. How did such a foolish man become so rich?"

"By caring for my herd," the swineherd said, raising his staff. "It is because of them that I have what I have. It is for them I must be willing to give it up."

The tiger leaped at the swineherd, and the two fought tooth and nail. Though the tiger was vicious, the swineherd did not give up, for he had his herd to protect. And when at last the two lay bloodied and broken on the jungle floor, it was impossible to know who had won and who had lost.

So the King of Death chose the victor, and took the tiger's soul. Then he helped the swineherd to his feet. "Why did you spare me?" the swineherd said, leaning on his staff, but the King of Death only smiled.

"Because I too care for my herd."

CHAPTER TWENTY-ONE

As I watch the message to Ayla flutter into the dark, my uncertainty returns. I hardly know the woman—how can I trust her? She had reminded me so much of Maman, but Maman herself had always warned me to keep my power a secret.

Never show, never tell, she used to say. But that was when the old ways were forbidden in Chakrana. Now I'm far from home, and there is no use hiding anymore. Soon enough, all of Aquitan will know.

Still, when a knock comes at the theater door, I half expect to see the entire armée when I open it. But Ayla herself stands on the doorstep, her face half hidden by the hood of a cloak. In the shadows, her expression is even more nervous than my own. She is no longer afraid for me, but afraid of me.

The look makes my heart hurt, but I reach for my own poise and paste on a smile. "Come in," I say, stepping back, and she follows slowly—carefully. Stepping through the door, she glances over my shoulder, right, then left, as though checking if I am alone.

Frowning, I watch her duck into the theater, peering at the empty seats. Then she squints up toward the balconies and the boxes. She returns to the lobby as I am closing the door. "Wait," she says, opening it again and beckoning to someone outside. Peeking out into the dark, I realize she has brought an armée after all, but they are not Aquitans. As she holds the door open, Chakrans file into the lobby. They too have hidden their faces with deep hoods or hats pulled low.

But as Ayla had taught me, I look at their hands and recognize the scars and calluses there. These are puppeteers and musicians—artists, like me. Some of them even carry leather cases at their sides, the right size and shape to hold Chakran instruments or tools to work leather.

They cluster behind Ayla, as though she is a shield, and I wonder how many of them she had welcomed—how many she had tried to protect with her poise and a well-placed word. Now, with the door shut against outsiders, she pushes back the hood of her cloak and draws something from the pocket. It is the letter I had sent, still folded.

"Show them," Ayla says to me. "Show them what you showed me."

I look at my audience, their expectant faces. Chakran faces. There is no scrim between us, nothing to hide behind—no way to pretend that my power is anything but what it is. So I take a deep breath and glance back at Ayla, at the letter on her palm. "Up," I say to the soul inside. The paper wings stir as the note takes wing, fluttering toward the coffered ceilings.

The audience gasps. Candlelight gleams in their eyes as they watch the note circle the chandeliers. Is that fear or awe on their faces? After two passes through the lobby, I send the letter toward the door of the theater. As it swoops down the aisle toward the stage, a few people break into a run to follow it. Laughing, I lead them on a chase up the other aisle. When the letter comes soaring back through the opposite door, I send it up once more toward the closest chandelier.

It circles once, twice, then dips toward the flame. I summon it back to my hand, the tail alight. Grabbing the letter with a flourish, I let it burn as I take a bow. The audience applauds, though I am the only one who can see the soul fly free.

Still, the soullight seems to shine in Ayla's eyes as she turns to her companions. "You see?" she says, her grin triumphant. "Fighter, artist, savior . . . nécromancien. How can we help?"

Her joy surprises me—she seems so unafraid. "It might be dangerous," I warn them. "I cannot guarantee Le Roi will enjoy the show."

"I'm sure I will," Ayla says, her hands going to the buttons at her throat. "It's bound to be unforgettable."

Before I can reply, she pulls off the heavy wool, revealing a Chakran sarong underneath. It's a lovely one, woven of purple silk, but what catches my eye are the tattoos that unfurl across her bare shoulders. They are black against the pale gold of her skin, like shadows on a scrim, like ink on a page. "You were a monk before you were a shadow player," I say, but she smiles.

"I am a monk *and* a shadow player. And if I ever come home, I will have a new sin to bear: cowardice. I am ready to put it behind me." Ayla tosses her cloak in a corner and cracks her knuckles, as though prepared to work. "Now. What do you need?"

She looks to me, her expression mirrored by the artists behind her: musicians and singers, fire tenders, puppeteers. "The play is the Shepherd . . . the Swineherd and the Tiger," I say slowly; there is recognition in their eyes. "But there will be some modifications. Do any of you know anyone who works at the boneyards?"

Several of the performers murmur, and a few nod. Then they all turn when a man speaks from the back of the crowd. "I do." His voice is deep and rich—the voice of a singer—but when he steps forward, I recognize him. He has wiped the sweat from his brow and the muck from his shoes, but he cannot clean the deep grime from his gnarled hands. This was the man I had seen on my way to the salon, when I had been too ashamed to meet his eyes. "I work there."

His words ring in the lobby like the deep tolling of a bell. I want to ask him what he did to be banished from the stage, how the king could bear to silence a voice like his. But I do not want to remind the others of the risks—nor do I want to think of them myself.

Instead, I take a deep breath and tell him what I need for the show. When he sets off into the night, the other performers get to work, some adjusting the lights as others unpack and tune their instruments. A painter starts on a poster for the easel outside the theater, and the singer reviews my changes to the original song. As the air rings with chatter and laughter and snippets of familiar music, the puppeteers wait. Some of them have their tools laid out on the stage—wire and paint and awls and gilding—but we are still waiting for the rest of our supplies.

I wait with them, and as the hours pass, I find myself trying to read the Old Chakran on Ayla's tattoos. Excessive pride . . . lack of caution . . . "Careless of the well-being of others," she adds when she catches me. "Deficient in compassion . . ."

"It's hard to believe," I say, embarrassed to be caught staring. But she only smiles, turning to face me.

"It's tempting to say that I was a different person then," she admits. "But I am the same person. I only try every day to do better than I am."

"I know that feeling," I say, returning her smile with a rueful one of my own. I can only imagine the sins I'd bear if I ever became a monk. Combative. Impulsive. Distracted. Obsessed. The words echo in my head as my thoughts begin to race around them. "What god do you serve?" I ask, trying to focus, but Ayla's smile falls away.

"I serve the King of Death," she says softly, and it takes everything in me not to recoil. Le Trépas serves the King of Death as well. But that is the only thing he and Ayla seem to have in common. Still, she is a good enough performer to recognize the tension in my expression. Her smile returns, sadder now. "Le Trépas has taken so much from all of us," she says. "I spent so long praying that someone would bring it back some day."

"Bring what back, exactly?" I say.

"The balance." She reaches out to touch my hand, squeezing my fingers in her own. "We have plenty of death, but not enough life, and precious little knowledge."

She looks like she's about to say more, but just then, one of the musicians comes racing up to the stage with a grin on his face. "Ayla! Jetta! Come eat!"

At the announcement, I tense; had the king sent a meal? Did he have spies hidden in the theater—or among the performers? Was he watching us make our preparations? But Ayla pats my hand and follows the musician, and then I smell it: the scent drifting through the theater. There is no way this meal was prepared in an Aquitan kitchen.

Reaching the lobby, I see the feast laid out on the marble

floor. Vegetable pancakes, curries, and a crispy fish to share—the flavors are both familiar and strange, as though the cook had to make do, but the dented brass platters and bowls remind me of home even more than the food. These dishes made the journey across the sea just as the rest of us did; they must have served many meals both there and here.

We sit cross-legged on the marble, like we all did at home. When everyone is done eating, I notice that all of us have left a little bit for the spirits, though I am the only one who can see them clustering. I watch them dip and swirl until the sound of a violin makes me turn.

My first wild thought is that it is Leo, but of course that's impossible. No—one of the musicians, who came prepared with her long-necked erhu and her worn guzheng, has also brought a violin. Her hand is not as confident as his—she is clearly still learning the Aquitan instrument. But as she plays, I hear another song: the refrain of the melody Leo had been working on the past few weeks. Haunting and tentative as the notes reach for resolution. Has he finished it yet?

I am so lost in my reverie that I jump when I feel a tap on my shoulder. Ayla is there at my side, and she nods toward the stage. Turning, I see men coming in the loading door, their backs bent under burlap sacks that shift and rattle on their shoulders.

As the king's servants had done with the fantouches from the salon, we bring the sacks full of bones to the stage. There is more space here, after all, and it will be easier to clean afterward. The bones themselves are old, stripped of flesh by worms and weather, and free of dirt. Still, there are so many to string together.

The puppeteers and I set to work, wiring the joints, stringing vertebrae like beads, arranging the tiny bones of feet and hands. It is painstaking work, but as Ayla said, art leaves its mark.

The work continues into the night. The others leave in small groups as they tire, but Ayla and I keep going till our fingers are raw and bleeding and the last bones are strung. Only then does she say her goodbyes, and I walk her, yawning, to the stage door.

"How can I repay you for your help?" I ask as she wraps her cloak around her shoulders, pulling her hood down to hide her face once more.

Her smile is even deeper than the shadows. "You can save me a seat."

"Front row," I promise, but she shakes her head.

"For this, I'd like to sit in the back," she says. "The performance will be a sight to see, but I'm most interested in the audience's reaction."

"Me too," I say fervently. She bows deeply, and I return the gesture. Then she starts off into the predawn light.

I squint at the sky—and the barest glimmer of dawn above the side street on the theater. Then I smother another yawn. I want nothing more than to leave as well—to go back to my rooms at the palais and the soft bed there. But I still have work to do.

On the stage, my fantouches wait, as lifeless as the dead. But in the theater, souls glimmer in the corners. So I return with bloody hands to the bones, and set to work building not an armée, but a cast.

ACT 3,
SCENE 22

Under cover of night, AKRA stalks through the now-empty streets of Nokhor Khat. Though the bleeding has stopped, the bullet wound in his side still aches, as does the pain in his heart.

Although he saw fresh clothes in the costume shop, AKRA hasn't bothered changing out of the bloody uniform. When he was a capitaine, a ruined shirt would have counted against him, but now it should only make it easier to slip in with the rest of the dead soldiers. Then he reaches the docks and curses. The pier is deserted, and the Prix de Guerre *is already halfway out into the bay.*

AKRA: Why can't you keep your own damn timetable?

He kicks something toward the water—a muddy shoe, lost or discarded in the riot. The docks are littered with similar items: hats and handkerchiefs, broken bowls or bottles of wine. Something catches his eye—a little fantouche in the shape of a man. A children's toy, too small for a stage, but carefully made, and lovingly worn.

Crouching, AKRA picks it up; the limbs of the puppet dangle from his hand, connected by black thread to slender sticks of bamboo. It is not unlike the toys he used to make for JETTA when she was small.

Setting the puppet down, AKRA gathers himself, gauging the distance across the dark water. The Prix de Guerre *hasn't yet reached the open sea—above the ship, steam floats in wispy tatters. It seems the soldiers were right about the ship being low on coal. Still, AKRA has never been a strong swimmer. He casts about the pier, but there are no boats left in the harbor. Reluctantly, he sighs, kneeling on the edge of the dock, feeling ridiculous as he calls into the deep.*

Come here, you . . . dragon.

Ignoring the bodies drifting around the pilings, he pats the surface of the water awkwardly, as though calling a dog.

Here, girl.

CAMREON had told him the dragon would obey him, but while he is used to giving orders to soldiers, he has never spoken to a fantouche before. Still, he waits, and soon enough,

he sees a sinuous ripple in the water, followed by the horns of
the skeletal head. As the creature rises out of the water, AKRA
scrambles to his feet. Then, cautiously, he steps off the dock,
swinging a leg over the bones of her neck.

The dragon turns her head to look back at him, as though
she is judging him with her hollow eyes. Settling down
between the ridged vertebrae, AKRA jerks his chin toward
the ship in the harbor.

Take me to the *Prix de Guerre.*
The dock creaks as the dragon climbs out of the water,
bunching her haunches to leap skyward, but AKRA puts a
frantic hand on her neck.
Down! In the water. So they don't see us coming.

Uncoiling, the dragon slips back into the bay, and AKRA
hunches down over her neck, holding his pistol over his head.

The night is quiet and the moon is slim. Goose bumps skitter
across AKRA's skin as the warm water of the harbor gives way
to the cooler currents sweeping in from the Hundred Days Sea.

The dragon swims quickly, her long tail undulating through
the water as she closes the distance to the Prix de Guerre. *Soon*
enough, they are in the shadow of the ship. Circling in the water,

AKRA looks for the best way to sneak aboard. The side is slick with algae and studded with barnacles, and the deck seems a mile away, but the dragon could easily bring him up.

Then, above the slow chug of the boilers, the monk's voice floats across the water as he calls to his soldiers.

LE TRÉPAS: We need to go faster! We'll be at sea for weeks at this pace.

He receives no answer—the dead aren't much for conversation. But AKRA can hear the sounds of the soldiers responding to his orders. Boots crossing the boards, the heave and saw of rope as they adjust the sails or turn the rudder or whatever it is they are doing on the deck above.

AKRA crouches lower in the water, hoping none of them happen to look over the side. He presses his hand to his wound. It is still tender. Bullets would not kill him, but given enough of them, he might wish they could.

Best to slip aboard unnoticed, but how? Then he sees the open windows of the captain's staterooms. From there he can get a look at what he's facing.

Holding tightly to the bones in the dragon's neck, AKRA urges her upward. The beast leaps lightly from the water to scramble up the side of the ship. Reaching the rear window, AKRA peers over the sill into the cabin. Then his eyes widen.

LEO is there, sitting cross-legged on the floor. He looks unhurt, and he isn't even bound. But the boy is deep in thought, using the nib of a fountain pen to scratch furiously at the polished wooden floor.

The fountain pen. When AKRA sees it, he scrambles over the sill, hissing at the pain in his rib as he slithers through the window.

AKRA: A little help?

LEO looks up, startled, as AKRA drops to the floor.

LEO: Akra. Mon dieu. I've never been so glad to see you in my life.

AKRA: I can say the same, though the bar is low enough to trip on. Give me that pen! We can use it to send the ship back to harbor.

AKRA snatches the pen, but LEO shakes his head.

LEO: It's empty.

AKRA: Oh.

AKRA frowns at the pen, then down at the marks LEO has carved into the wooden floor. Words and notes, like music.

What the hell? Never mind. Come on, the dragon's waiting. At the very least we can get you out of here.

LEO: I . . . can't.

AKRA: Are you hurt?

LEO: Not exactly.

LEO extends his hand, palm up. AKRA reaches for him, intending to pull him to his feet, then stops when he sees the mark on LEO's wrist. The blood is flaking as it dries, but even so, AKRA can make out two symbols: death, and life.

At least, not anymore.

A Good Time

music and lyrics by
Mei Rath

Sultry swing, not too slow ($\quad$ = 64)

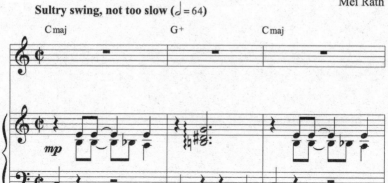

Turn down the lights,   we just___ need a spark.

In sha - dows ev - 'ry truth can

be re - vealed. Let oth - ers

won - der what hap - pens in the dark.____

Two can keep a se - cret if their lips are

sealed. Al-though we don't have much

time, we'll have such a good time. We'll

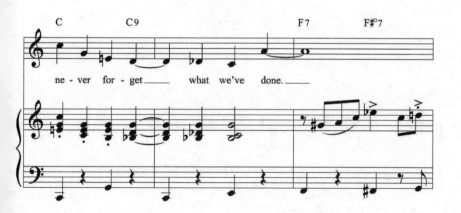

ne-ver for-get what we've done.

It goes by so fast,_____ I'm a-

fraid it's the last_____ time, So let's have the

Tempo primo ($\boldsymbol{\mathethtt{\,}}$ = 64)

best kind__ of fun.

Don't beg or ar - gue, don't tell me it's

Freely

wrong. Just give me a

Somewhat faster ($\quad$ = 82)

rea - son____ to stay._____ We

never have much time, so make it a good

time. We'll nev - er for - get what we've done.

Oh, Time goes so fast,

best kind_____ of...

A little slower ($\d = 73$)

fun.

ACT 3,

SCENE 23

Inside the Ruby Palace. In a courtyard antechamber, a decorative bridge arches over a reflecting pond. But the servants fled when LE TRÉPAS came, and there is no one left to tend the garden. The once-clear water has gone green with algae, and mosquitoes whine in the air as overhanging orchids drop spent blooms onto the path. Even worse are the flies. LE TRÉPAS had hidden his armée of the dead inside the palace walls, and though they have gone to the docks, the stench of rot still lingers.

Still, the rebels do not shy away. CAMREON leads the girls deeper into the palace, surprisingly sure-footed in his dress and silk slippers—a good disguise can be a more powerful weapon than a gun. CHEEKY and TIA follow him across the bridge, down a path, and through a set of wide double doors.

Beyond, the rebels find a sitting room where pillows and carpets are scattered messily across the wide floor. Past that, another antechamber holds an octagonal table big enough to seat two dozen people for meals or meetings. Now it holds only a single place setting and the remains of a half-eaten dinner. CHEEKY frowns at the line of ants marching away from the plate.

CHEEKY: I guess dead men don't do dishes.

TIA: So same as live men, then.

CAMREON: Shh.

Lightly, CAMREON approaches the next door: an imposing entry, enameled black and decorated with a bronze dragon ascending.

This is the bedchamber. Last chance to back out.

TIA chews her lip, looking at CHEEKY, but the showgirl puts on a brave face.

CHEEKY: I'm looking forward to sending our bill to the treasury when this is all over.

TIA: Just tell me you're not going to itemize it.

CHEEKY snorts a laugh, but CAMREON doesn't smile as he reaches for the handle. A moment passes, then another. CHEEKY narrows her eyes, but her look is not unkind.

CHEEKY: Last chance to back out.

Now a smile touches CAMREON's lips. He takes a deep breath, then opens the door.

Moonlight spills across the darkened room, illuminating the gilded furnishings: a chaise lounge, an imported dresser, a velvet-draped bed. Aquitan furnishings, strangely out of place in the Ruby Palace. But the drapes are drawn back, and the bed is empty.

TIA: Where is he?

CHEEKY: Shh.

She holds up a finger, cocking her head. In the soft dark silence, a distant sound comes: music. The notes are gentle . . . halting. A section of a song that fades, then starts over.

I used to dance to this song.

TIA: I remember.

CHEEKY: Of course you do. I'm unforgettable.

CHEEKY grins, but something about the music has thrown her off. She starts across the room, toward the sound of the piano, but she hesitates at the far door, the way an actor would when about to step onto the stage. As CAMREON and TIA watch, she straightens her shoulders and dons a little smile—hopeful, appealing. Then she opens the door, and the music flows through.

On the other side of the door, she finds a study. Dusty bookshelves line the wall, and a desk has been pushed aside to make room for new instruments: a harp shining soft gold in the corner, a fine violin on a silver stand, and a grand piano, all polished ebony and gold fittings. Imported Aquitan instruments. They have fallen out of tune in the local humidity, and there are no servants left to fix the pitch.

RAIK is sitting at the piano, a half-empty bottle of champagne on the lid. His fingers skip over the keys, and he seems not to hear the sour notes. But when CHEEKY steps into the room, his hands go still.

RAIK: You came back.

CHEEKY: How could I stay away?

RAIK's face hardens.

RAIK: Is your soldier done with you?

CHEEKY: He was a mistake. We all make them.

She approaches, leaning in over the keys, and plays the next few notes.

RAIK: You think I don't know that?

CHEEKY: Au contraire. I think you can relate.

She sits down beside him to play the next line. RAIK leans into her warmth, taking a deep breath of her perfume.

When we were in the jungle, all you talked about was coming back to Nokhor Khat. You painted it like a picture in my head. The city full of life and beauty. Servants at your beck and call in the palace. You could go out to a show, or play cards at the gambling house—

Her finger lands on a sour key, and she winces.

But that's not what I saw when I came here.

RAIK: That's not my fault.

CHEEKY: I know. It's your brother's. But you're the one stuck here in an empty palace that still smells of corpses, with the country crumbling and the champagne harder and harder to get—

Slamming his hands down on the keys in a discordant clang, RAIK turns to her.

RAIK: And what do you expect me to do about any of that?

CHEEKY: Nothing.

Gently she takes his hands.

Let him clean up the mess.

RAIK: Who?

CHEEKY: Your brother. And why shouldn't he? It's his fault.

RAIK frowns as the wheels turn in his head.

RAIK: How do you know he would?

CHEEKY: It's what you talked about, isn't it? Before he persuaded you to leave the palace and join the rebellion. The only difference now is that you wouldn't even have to be a figurehead. All of the fun, none of the work. He wants the throne, doesn't he? Let him have it.

RAIK *stares at her, still suspicious, but she returns his gaze with deep admiration in her own eyes.*

RAIK: And what do you want?

CHEEKY: To stay by your side, as long as you'll have me.

RAIK: Is that so?

RAIK *searches her face, looking for the lie. Then, slowly, he nods. But as she leans closer for a kiss, his hand goes to his pocket.*

Then you should have no trouble letting me mark you.

CHEEKY: Mark . . . me?

RAIK: So I know you can't run off again.

He pulls out a slender length of brass—the fountain pen, full of Jetta's blood—that he ripped from CAMREON's hand on the steps of the palace. CHEEKY's eyes widen, but she struggles for composure, hiding her alarm.

CHEEKY: You want to make me a fantouche?

RAIK: So you'll stay with me. Don't you want to stay with me, Cheeky?

CHEEKY: Of course I do! But . . . isn't it better that I want to, than that you make me?

RAIK: It's better to know you won't betray me again.

He takes her hand, but she draws back, trying to laugh.

CHEEKY: It only works on the dead, Raik.

He grips her wrist harder, showing his teeth.

RAIK: You're dead either way.

He raises the pen in his fist, as though to stab her with it, but she scrambles over the back of the bench, tripping over the train of her dress. He grabs her ankle and she lashes out with her foot, kicking free. Tearing the violin from the stand, she swings it at him—a lover and a fighter. RAIK wrenches the instrument out of her hand, bringing it down like a club. CHEEKY has just enough time to get her hands over her head before the violin splinters over her shoulders. The girl collapses, dazed, as RAIK raises the pen again. But hearing the commotion, TIA and CAMREON burst through the door.

TIA: Cheeky!

TIA rushes to her friend's side, standing between RAIK and the girl.

RAIK: Tia? Get out, or you're next. And who the hell are you—

When RAIK meets his brother's eyes, his fury deepens.

You.

He turns to CAMREON, holding the pen like a dagger.

Of course you're behind this.

CAMREON puts his hands out, palms open, trying to calm his brother.

CAMREON: It's what's best for the country, Raik. And for the both of us. You never wanted to rule.

RAIK: And did you think that meant I wanted to watch you do it?

RAIK takes another step toward him, raising the pen.

Who am I, if I'm not the king?

CAMREON: You're my brother.

RAIK: Not anymore. Not after you abandoned me.

CAMREON's face twists.

CAMREON: I thought you were dead. It was so dark, there was blood everywhere—

RAIK: Not in the cave!

His shout echoes in the room, startling CAMREON into silence.

When we were children. After La Victoire. My whole life! While you were out becoming the Tiger, and the Aquitans made me into *this.*

He grips his white shirt—an Aquitan shirt—then flings his hand around the room, and all the imported treasures there.

Their puppet. The Boy King.

RAIK's lip curls, and he gestures to CAMREON's silk dress.

Do you know what it feels like for the whole country to think you're a better man than me?

CAMREON's eyes go wide, but before he can respond, RAIK lunges, pen in hand. CAM catches him by the wrist. The two grapple, but RAIK is taller, stronger. Driving CAMREON back against the wall, RAIK's arm shakes as he presses the pen ever closer, till the brass nib is inches from the Tiger's face.

But TIA scrambles to her feet, grabbing the bottle of champagne. Lifting it by the neck, she charges at RAIK with a cry, champagne spilling across the floor. At the sound of her voice, the Boy King half turns. The distraction is all CAMREON needs. The Tiger ducks, letting go of RAIK's hand. Suddenly off-balance, the Boy King falls forward, stumbling into the plaster wall. But when he falls back, dazed, blood is pouring from his right eye. The back of the pen has been driven deep into the socket.

RAIK staggers forward, his limbs twitching like a broken puppet. CAMREON catches him, easing him to the carpet.

CAMREON: Raik . . .

The Boy King's lips move, but no sound comes out. Blood trickles from his ruined eye like tears; his other eye glazes over, then closes. For a moment, the only sound is CAMREON's ragged breathing. Then he kneels beside his brother, pressing his fingers to the king's throat. Finding no pulse, he raises his hand to cup his brother's bloody cheek. TIA comes to his side, still clutching the neck of the bottle.

TIA: Are you okay?

CAM: Yes.

The word is clipped. The Tiger swallows, but TIA doesn't point out the lie.

Is Cheeky?

CHEEKY: I will be.

The girl pushes herself to her feet, wincing, her hand going to the back of her head.

I knew I should have gone with the sarong.

She comes to his side, looking at RAIK, then looks away quickly.

What are we going to do now?

CAMREON takes a deep breath, trying to gather his thoughts, but he can't take his eyes off his brother's face.

CAMREON: We . . . we lock the door. Look for weapons. The guards won't be expecting us to come out till morning.

CHEEKY: And what happens in the morning?

CAMREON: I don't know!

CHEEKY draws back, eyes wide. This is the first time she has ever heard CAMREON raise his voice. The Tiger too seems surprised by his own outburst, but TIA puts her hand on his shoulder.

TIA: I do.

When his hand comes up to cover hers, she squeezes CAM's fingers, then pulls him to his feet.

There should be clothes in Raik's closet. Something kingly. Go change.

She pushes CAM toward the bedchamber, but he hesitates.

CAMREON: And then?

TIA: And then when the rest of the capital wakes up, they find you on the throne.

CAMREON: What about my brother?

TIA hesitates, looking at the Boy King's body—at the bloody pen still protruding from his eye. But CHEEKY is the one to speak, her voice tentative as she creates the narrative.

CHEEKY: He finally succumbed to his wounds from the battle at the temple.

CAMREON: No one's going to believe that.

TIA: It doesn't matter what they believe. It matters what you do. What you show them. Who you are. Right?

CAMREON: Right.

CAMREON takes a deep breath, collecting himself.

Right.

TIA: Now go. Get dressed.

CAMREON nods, turning toward the bedchamber, leaving the girls with RAIK's body. The girls share a look, then CHEEKY nods down at the bloody pen, still protruding from the corpse's eye.

CHEEKY: You know we need to get that back. Just in case we need it.

TIA: We? I saved your life.

CHEEKY: I loaned you my ostrich feathers.

TIA gives her a look.

TIA: That was two years ago!

CHEEKY: I still never got them back.

TIA stares at her for a moment, then starts laughing. CHEEKY joins her, and soon the two girls are lost in wave after wave of hysterical laughter that turns too suddenly into tears.

This is horrible. This is so horrible.

TIA: I know.

They cling to each other for a long time, and it is hard to tell which is preventing the other from falling. At last, their sobs subside into sniffles, and CHEEKY pulls back, taking a deep shuddering breath.

CHEEKY: Is there any champagne left?

TIA picks up the bottle she had hit RAIK with, tipping it

upside down. A tiny drop falls out onto the carpet.

CHEEKY: Figures. All right. On three.

Taking another breath, she kneels beside the body, reaching with trembling hands for the pen.

One . . . two . . . two and a half . . .

Her fingers hover near the pen, so TIA reaches out, grabbing the pen herself and jerking it free.

TIA: Three.

CHAPTER

TWENTY-FOUR

Any shadow player knows that a show starts long before the curtain rises.

An audience arrives at the theater with expectations: what play they'll see, or what troupe is behind the scrim. More sophisticated playgoers will know a particular troupe's usual style, and an experienced troupe always knows how to use those expectations—and when to break them. Know your enemy, the saying goes, but in the theater, it's "Know your audience."

Of course, one reason my arrival has caused such a stir is that no one in Aquitan yet knows me, which is why the billing is so important. I have to tell them what to expect.

As they fill the seats, I can hear the word sparkling in the air like the light of the chandeliers: *nécromancien*. Just as it says in the poster in the lobby. But the idea seems to thrill the Aquitans. Of course, there is a difference between knowledge and experience.

I myself am surprisingly calm. Usually I have to struggle for composure before a show, but as I wait backstage, my palms are dry and my thoughts are measured. When I risk a peek around the scrim, even the sight of the seats—so many, and so full, all the way up to the balcony—does not ruffle my calm.

Then I catch sight of Le Roi. He sits in the front row, where few can see his face, though I have a clear view. But he is a performer in his own right, and I cannot read his expression. What does he think of my billing? I suppose we'll know soon enough.

Ducking back behind the scrim, I nod to the musicians in the wings. They lift their instruments and begin tuning. The first notes make my heart beat faster, as does the expectant hush that follows. They are familiar sounds—the fading whispers of conversations. The gentle percussion of feet and chairs. The soft rhythm of breath and blood, usually imperceptible, that builds to a thrum when crowds gather.

These are the sounds that have always centered me, but now, at the eleventh hour, doubt creeps in. What if the show goes awry, if the audience deems me a charlatan, or Le Roi brands me a traitor? What would happen to me—to the rebellion, to Leo on the *Prix de Guerre* and Theodora in the sanatorium? What would happen to my country—and my countrymen? Peering into the shadows of the wings, I meet the singer's eyes. Davri is his name, and he had told me it had been years since he'd sung on stage. Will he ever do it again after tonight?

For him . . . for me . . . for all of us, the show must go well. But no matter what, the show must go on.

So when the musicians fall silent, I step from the wings to the center of the stage, careful not to trip over my fantouches. I have laid them out between the scrim and the fire bowl—or rather, the gas lamp. It's half my height, with a mirrored backing, and all I have to do is turn a knob to raise the flames. Still, as I kneel in front of it, I close my eyes, imaging the smell of woodsmoke like we used back home. The flames rise before me, and the heat makes the burn scar on my shoulder tingle. Shadow play has always been a dangerous profession. Only tonight, it's not because of the flame.

Still on my knees, I turn back downstage, keeping my own shadow off the scrim. The musicians know the signal, and after a moment, the first strains of music rise with the light.

The audience should know the song well, though as with all old stories, the joy is not in how the story ends, but in how it's told. Indeed, most of the time, shadow plays are performed in Chakran; the Aquitan audience doesn't even understand the language. They have only memorized what should happen without understanding why.

But now, when Davri joins in, he sings in Aquitan. I have translated the words with care, because I want to be sure the audience finally knows the real story.

"In the days when our ancestors were young," he begins, his voice like a deep river. I can feel the air move through the theater as the audience gasps at the sound. "There was a brave shepherd who tended his flock."

My heart beating in time with the rhythm, I raise my first fantouche: not a shepherd, nor a swineherd, but a king.

The skeleton stands on the stage before me, bare but for a crown of brass and glass. On the other side of the scrim, the audience cannot see the stark expression of the skull, nor hear the rattle of his bones over the music. Still, I can sense their sudden unease. These shadows are nothing like what they expected.

"Under his eye, his flock grew and grew. . . ."

Another skeleton rises, and another, each bowing deeply to the king. These, we have dressed in costume—a gown, a suit, a hat, a parasol. But I keep them in profile, so the firelight outlines the disturbing silhouette of their noseless faces. Now I can hear the audience shifting in their seats.

"Until the day a tiger came prowling—"

I raise another fantouche, this one crafted in the traditional style. Painted leather scraped so thin the light shines through, delicate joints that make the graceful movements almost lifelike . . . but not the tiger puppet they expect. The tiger I had borrowed from the king is still in the silk bag backstage. Instead, I have borrowed Ayla's version of the King of Death. I would swear she crafted him after Le Trépas, down to the scraped lines of scars over where his heart would be.

"To devour them one by one."

The King of Death extends a graceful hand, lifting the king's subjects to their feet. Then the skeletons bow to him, and they do not get up again.

Now, the two kings face each other alone in silhouette, as would the Tiger and the Shepherd, if I were actually telling that story. But instead of the battle that would normally ensue, the music stops suddenly, and my own voice rings out as the skeletal king bows too, prostrating himself on the ground.

"And the shepherd did nothing."

The crowd erupts at the insult, gasping and jeering, but I cannot see their reaction from behind the scrim. They cannot see my fantouches either—not the way they should. So I step forward into the light, my own silhouette looming, and lift my hand. The long shadows of my fingertips reach for the top of the scrim, and I murmur to the soul I'd put into the silk as my shadow tears it down.

Obligingly, the silk drape falls in a rippling heap, leaving me face-to-face with the startled audience. Their wide eyes reflect the firelight as they look from me to the fantouche of the King of Death, held up without stick or string.

I can see the questions in their faces. How is it done? What is the trick?

And other questions too. How dare she? Is this supposed to happen?

They do not know how to respond, so they wait,

breathless, for a cue from Le Roi. On his face is an expression of disdain, barely concealing the anger underneath. "What is the meaning of this?" he says.

I had thought the crowd was silent before, but as they wait for my answer, it's as though they've stopped breathing. "I promised you a show like you've never seen," I reply. "So I decided to show you who you are."

"This is not a show," Le Roi replies, standing to leave. "It's a snub."

"You haven't seen the finale," I call after him, but the king doesn't turn back. The audience too stands, following his lead, but the show is far from over. So I send the fantouche of the King of Death down the steps and into the aisle to intercept Le Roi.

The audience murmurs again, louder now, but if Le Roi is wondering how my fantouche works, he hides it well. Reaching out, he snatches the leather puppet from its feet and tosses it aside. But I am done with the leather fantouches. Instead I call to the next: my false shepherd, my skeleton king.

In a rattle of bones, it rises, the glass jewel of the wire crown shining in the light of the fire. The gossamer robes we had fashioned to dress him shimmer over the old bones, and the audience gasps again, this time in horror. Le Roi turns back at the sound, and I see the look in his eyes as I raise another fantouche, and another. There is awe on his face—and fear—as he watches the fourth skeleton rise, then the fifth.

The others join them—my whole cast, ready for their turn on stage. The word is rippling through the audience again—*nécromancien, nécromancien*—but the condescension has been replaced with desperation. Still, they turn to the king for a cue, but it is no longer his show.

"Direct from Chakrana," I say, pitching my voice to carry, and in the silence of the living, I can hear the clacking bones of the dead. "Never before seen in Aquitan. And if you give me my payment, Theodora and I will be on our way home and you'll never have to see them again."

Le Roi glances from me to my cast, weighing his options—still hoping, perhaps, that this is all some charlatan's trick. Or does he hope to trick *me*? "Come then," he says. "Let me take you to the salon to claim your reward."

"No need," I say. "It's waiting outside."

He raises an eyebrow. But I only step down from the stage to join him in the aisle, followed by my cast of skeletons, and he has to hurry to join me. Behind my entourage, the audience rushes into the aisles to follow.

Leading the impromptu parade into the lobby, I throw the doors open to the night. There, on the wide stone stairs, the skeleton of the griffin is waiting. I had summoned the creature just before the show started, in case I needed to make a quick exit. Now, the beast cocks his head as I approach, the book held lightly in his curved beak.

Le Roi stops on the steps when he sees the creature, and now the anger on his face falls away. "The avions," he says quietly. "It isn't engineering that makes them fly."

"No, Your Majesty," I confirm. Turning to give him a little bow, I see what looks like the entire audience on the steps behind us. But it is whispers that ring in their ears, instead of music—*nécromancien, nécromancien*—and the terror has been replaced with awe. I take a breath, looking back at the king: perhaps a private conversation is in order. "Will you join me at Les Chanceux?"

I hold out my hand, aware of the audience. After a moment, Le Roi takes it.

I pull him up after me on the back of the griffin, and we spring into the air as the crowd gasps. Then, as we wheel away from the theater, applause breaks out behind us.

The evening streets are not crowded, but neither are

they empty, and as we soar higher and higher over Lephare, passersby gawk. But I wish I could see Le Roi's face—try to read his expression. Does the griffin delight him, or is he only afraid of falling to the hard earth below? When he speaks at last, his voice is carefully soft, even over the rushing wind. "You were right," he says. "You should stay in Aquitan."

"I am needed in Chakrana, Your Majesty," I say. "As is Theodora."

"Whatever they pay," the king says quickly. "I'll double it."

I can't help but laugh; rebellion pays even worse than art, but I can't tell the king that. "The wealth you offer is stolen."

To my surprise, he thrusts something out. The crown— gleaming gold and sapphire blue. "Take it," the king insists, pressing it into my hands. "Anything else. Everything else. The contents of the jewel room if you stay to work for me."

I look down at the crown in my hands. It is so heavy. How can he bear the weight? The jewel seems to wink at me, the color of vengeance. Le Roi has taken so much, and yet he has nothing to offer that can truly tempt me. Shaking my head, I hand the crown back. "I can't stay," I say. "But my fantouches will."

"The skeletons?" Le Roi shifts behind me, and his voice takes on a hint of uncertainty. "And . . . what will they do?"

"Nothing, Your Majesty," I say mildly. "Unless I order otherwise. Of course you could always send them to Chakrana aboard a ship, along with any other Chakrans who wish to come home."

"A ship," the king repeats dully. "I see."

"Don't worry, Your Majesty. We'll send it back with any refugees that may wish to return to Aquitan. It is a good start to the new alliance between our countries."

"Indeed," Le Roi says. "With the rebel king, I suppose."

"And the nécromancien," I say as the griffin begins to circle lower. Have we reached the springs already? "But I'll leave it to Theodora to discuss the details. She's always been a better diplomat than me."

"I'm very much looking forward to those discussions," the king lies, but I hardly hear him. Instead, I am scanning the ground below.

Despite having the Keeper's book and the king's offers, there is a deeper thrill at the thought of seeing Les Chanceux. The spring is the source for the treatment of my malheur—the inspiration for my desire to come to Aquitan in the first place. With the wind in my hair, I wait for my first glimpse of the hazy blue water and the craggy limestone rocks. I half imagine the women in the painting will still be there, bathing. But all I see as we descend is a circular courtyard before a tall limestone building.

"Where is Les Chanceux?" I murmur to the king, but he nods down at the sanatorium.

"If you set down in the courtyard, I'll have Theodora brought out," he says.

"Bien," I say as we circle lower, still scanning the terrain, but there is no sign of the pool in the painting.

The griffin touches down on the wide cobbled court, and the king dismounts on his own. Without his servants and his audience to see, he doesn't bother with fanfare as he strides up the steps. I do not follow him; part of me still fears a trick, or that I will be locked inside if I get too close.

The other part of me still wonders where the spring is hidden. I turn the griffin in a slow circle, her claws clacking on the stones. Then I see it, dead center—and it is nothing like I expected. The craggy stone pool has been cleared and tamed, replaced by a carved limestone basin with a little font inside. Something gleams in the lamplight . . . a little brass plaque set into the rim. Nudging my mount closer, I can just make it out: LES CHANCEUX.

What has become of the springs in the painting? The blue waters, the hazy air, the languid bathers—had they ever existed outside the frame, or was it all an artist's vision? Putting my hand beneath the trickle of water, I lift my cupped palms to my lips, tasting the bitter tang of the minerals inside. That, at least, is the same.

"Jetta?"

Turning, I see Theodora flying down the steps, her blond curls disheveled. Her uncle walks behind her, but for a moment, I see not Le Roi, but his own half-brother—Theodora's father, the Shepherd of Chakrana, a country with no sheep.

He stops halfway through the courtyard, as if he is not eager to continue our negotiations, and I don't blame him. As Theodora approaches, I can see the pink spots on her cheeks that always appear when she is furious, and I wonder what she said to him inside. But when she reaches my side, the anger on her face fades into relief. "You have no idea how glad I am to see you," she says fervently. Then she hesitates, looking at the griffin. Her eyes widen when she sees the book still clamped in his beak. "Is that . . . ?"

"It is," I say as she reaches for the book. Gently, the griffin releases it. Clutching the book tightly, she climbs up behind me. "I have the elixir too," I add; the flask is still heavy in my pocket. "And your uncle should be sending a ship soon enough."

"Then let's go home." Theodora says, and the word makes my own heart ache. Beneath us, the griffin crouches, ready to fly, but before I can give the order, something flits past my cheek.

A night moth? No—a note. It flutters back, a folded piece of paper like the one I'd sent to Ayla. But I had burned that letter in the lobby of the theater. Where did this one come from? Camreon? Leo? But why hadn't they just asked Akra to speak to me? Shame grows in my breast as I remember our argument. Taking the letter, I unfold it, dreading the contents, but they are even worse than I could have imagined.

Cursing, I stuff the letter in my pocket and push the griffin into the sky. The bone wings beat, made frantic by my own fear. "What is it?" Theodora says.

I brace myself to say the words, to make them alarmingly real. "Le Trépas has Leo."

If you will not come for your
elixir, come for your moitié,
or I will send him after you.

ACT 3,

SCENE 25

In the cabin of the Prix de Guerre. *LEO still sits, cross-legged, as AKRA paces across the floor, thinking.*

LEO: It's strange. I don't even remember dying.

AKRA: Be glad of that.

AKRA shudders at his own memories.

Why would you be so reckless?

LEO: Le Trépas took Jetta's blood from me. I had to get it back.

AKRA glances at the mark on LEO's wrist.

AKRA: And so you did.

LEO: He was going to use it to get us to Aquitan faster.

AKRA: So?

LEO: When we get there, he's going to turn the Aquitans belowdecks into an armée of the dead. I saved their lives, Akra.

AKRA: You bought them some time.

LEO: That's all any of us have. Time.

LEO looks back at the bloody mark on his wrist.

Some of it stolen.

He sighs, then runs a hand over the carvings on the floor.

At least I finished her song.

AKRA *(gruffly)*: Well. That's something.

AKRA looks down at the carvings as well, then looks away, embarrassed.

Did Le Trépas give you any other orders?

LEO: No. Just to stay. Like a dog. I hate it.

AKRA: Tell me about it.

LEO: Does Jetta do this to you?

AKRA: No.

He hesitates.

For the most part. All right . . .

Reluctantly, he picks up the frayed rope from the floor, but LEO takes it eagerly.

New plan. Tie your feet and hands, just in case the monk gets any ideas. Then when Jetta gets here, she can . . .

He trails off, waves his hands vaguely. LEO quirks an eyebrow as he wraps the rope around his own ankles.

LEO: Kill me?

AKRA: Bring you back.

LEO: Ha. No. Not again.

He shakes his head.

I'm sorry. I . . . I don't know how you do it.

AKRA: You get used to anything, if it's a matter of life or death.

LEO: But death is just a part of life.

AKRA starts pacing again, as though his own memories are chasing after him: the way it felt when his soul returned to his empty body, like coming home to find the front door hanging open and a cold wind sweeping leaves across the floor.

AKRA: Take it up with Jetta.

LEO grits his teeth, then double knots the ropes at his feet. Then he starts on his wrists, frowning.

LEO: A little help?

But AKRA has stopped to look through the rear window. A wide silver wake churns behind the ship.

AKRA: That's strange.

LEO: What is it?

AKRA: We're moving faster now.

AKRA cocks his head, but the sound of the boiler is no louder than it was. Crossing the cabin, AKRA approaches the door, peering through the tiny window. Where hundreds of soldiers had stood on the deck, there are only a few dozen remaining. At their feet, coils of rope lie in puddles of salt spray and old blood. As he watches, the soldiers tie themselves into harnesses attached at various points to the bow, then climb in silence over the edge to drop into the dark water below.

AKRA: Le Trépas has his soldiers pulling the ship. Why does he need to go so fast?

LEO: To find Jetta?

AKRA: Or to protect the book.

LEO: How fast can the dead really swim?

AKRA: Fast enough.

AKRA's stomach sinks as two soldiers appear, dragging a living prisoner between them.

Especially if they're still alive when they go into the water.

CHAPTER TWENTY-SIX

Speeding over the Hundred Days Sea on the bone wings of the griffin, I scan the horizon for the first glimpse of land. We've been flying for hours, but the ocean is as wide as the night is long. Below, the dark water swirls with souls like stars, and my own stomach churns with worry over Leo.

"Any word from your brother?" Theodora asks, as she has at least twice an hour since we got Le Trépas's note.

I shake my head. "Not yet."

"Maybe we should have stopped for a pen," Theodora says—also not for the first time. Her hand goes to her own pocket; she's put the Book of Knowledge there for safekeeping. I explained to her how it works, but there is no way to get ink now that we're far out over the Hundred Days Sea. I focus on the horizon instead as Theodora shifts behind me. "Still no word from your brother?" she asks again.

"I've tried calling out for him," I say, exasperated. "But he can't hear me unless he's already listening."

"What if you order him to respond?"

"What? No," I say quickly. "I . . . can't do that."

"These are extenuating circumstances," Theodora says. "He needs to know we're coming. And we need to know they're both still alive."

I stiffen at the thought—in my fear over Leo, I hadn't considered that Akra too was at risk. He had survived a storm of bullets, a shot to the heart—but my blood could still kill him, and by his letter, I know that Le Trépas has my blood at his fingertips. If the old monk pulled Akra's soul from his body, I would never see my brother alive again. I stare down at the swirling sea, then take a breath to speak. "Akra," I say, as soft as an apology. "Talk to me. Please."

For a moment, the only sound is the wind in my ears. Then his voice comes, and the first word is a curse. "What do you want?"

"Theodora and I were worried about you," I say, but he snorts.

"Me, or Leo?"

I can't help myself; at the mention of Leo's name, my heart quickens. "Both of you. Have you found him yet?"

"We're together in the cabin of the *Prix de Guerre*," Akra says, and I sag in relief.

"He's alive," I say, and behind me, Theodora sighs.

"Thank the gods," she says. "And . . . Xavier?"

I repeat the question to Akra, but he hesitates before answering. "The general is beyond the monk's reach," my brother says at last, and I can't help the relief that I feel. I have no sympathy for Xavier Legarde, but the horror of seeing him raised was not easy for Leo or Theodora. "Unfortunately, the rest of us aren't so lucky."

My relief vanishes. "What happened?"

"The ship has left port," Akra says slowly. "Le Trépas is aboard."

"Probably coming to find me," I say. "I got a note from him."

Akra's response is careful. "What did it say?"

"He told me he had Leo," I say. "I'm glad to know he's safe with you."

"Right," Akra says, his voice gruff. His tone gives me pause, but behind me, Theodora leans close over my shoulder.

"Is that the ship there?" The girl points at a dark tide on the horizon—the soulless depth of a bottomless hole—and I see it too now. The *Prix de Guerre*. But there are lights on the bow—a few torches, gleaming. That must be what drew Theodora's eye. In the flickering light, I can make out the silhouettes of people gathered there. Theodora lowers her hand. "What are they doing?"

"I'm not sure." Speeding toward the ship, the souls around me fall away, too afraid of Le Trépas to follow. I try to make out the scene in the dark—the white water like a wake before the ship, the figures struggling on the bow. Then I gasp as a man falls, arms windmilling, into the dark water. "They're pushing people off the ship?"

"Where are you?" Akra says, confusion in his voice.

"I can see the *Prix de Guerre*," I say, my heart pounding—the monk is there too, on the bow. "I can see Le Trépas."

"I thought you were still in Aquitan!" Akra's own voice is panicked, but I am staring in horror as the soldiers drag another man to the bow.

"No . . ." Despite the smell of salt spray and the wind in

my face, for a moment, I am back in the paddies at Malao. But this prisoner is alive—for now. He struggles as they tie a harness around his waist. "I'm here," I say through my teeth. "I'm going to stop him."

"But what's the plan?" Akra's voice is sharp. "You can't just rush in again!"

Trying to focus, I tear my eyes away from the soldiers. "Theodora, you stay with the griffin," I say, loud enough for both her and Akra to hear. "Take the book to Nokhor Khat. I'll get to the ship and deal with Le Trépas."

"Just like that?" Akra snorts again. "There are no souls here for you to use. You don't even have a gun, do you?"

"Don't you?"

"Me and the other dead soldiers," Akra says. I grit my teeth, but my thoughts have scattered again, fleeing like the spirits as we draw ever closer to Le Trépas. A gun won't work, anyway. How will I kill a man with no soul? I have to find his soul first—bring it back to his body. That's what the Keeper told me. Where would Le Trépas have hidden it? I had thought we'd have more time to figure it out.

Something nags at the back of my mind . . . something like the answer. Know your enemy and know yourself. I know Le Trépas, don't I? I should know this.

Then, in a flash—clarity. I don't need to know where it is. The monk himself had taught me how to find it: how to rip old souls from fresh bodies. How to call them back from wherever they'd gone. All I need is a drop of his blood.

"Does the cabin door lock?" I call to Akra.

"It should," he replies.

"Can you shoot him, then shut yourselves inside?"

"Of course," my brother says. "But it won't kill him, will it?"

I scoff, disbelieving. "You sound worried that it might."

"No," Akra says quickly. "It's just . . . the door won't hold forever."

"All I need is his blood," I say. "It won't take long."

"You sound a lot more sure than I feel," Akra says, and I can't help but smile.

"I'm playing my role," I say. "Can you play yours?"

"I have four bullets left. Just give me the cue. Wait," he says then, hesitating. "Leo wants me to tell you something."

"Leo?" I say, my heart quickening. At my back, Theodora stiffens. "What is it?"

"He says . . . he says he finished your song."

I can't help it—I laugh. "I can't wait to hear it."

Behind me, Theodora taps me on the shoulder. "Tell my brother I love him, will you?"

"Theodora sends Leo her love," I say to Akra, and my own brother groans.

"I'm more ready to die than ever," he says, and I laugh again. Then I push the griffin down toward the ship.

The night is deep, the moonlight thin, but if the monk were only to look up, he would surely see us silhouetted against the sky. But he is too focused on the soldiers' work at the bow, so I take a deep breath and call out in my best stage voice. "Le Trépas!"

His eyes flash white in the dark as he sees me, but Akra knows a cue when he hears one. At the stern, the cabin door swings wide. Over the sound of the waves, a gunshot rings out, then another. Le Trépas stumbles, falling to one knee. The monk whirls, furious, sending his soldiers toward the cabin as Akra ducks back inside and shuts the door. The dead men crowd close, hammering at the door with bloody hands.

If they can break through to the cabin, I have no doubt they'll tear my brother and Leo to pieces. I need to hurry. Pushing the griffin lower, I leap from her back, rolling as I land. When I gain my footing, I catch a glimpse of Theodora's pale face as the skeletal beast carries her off. "Keep her safe," I shout as the creature wheels away. "Take her to Nokhor Khat!"

At the sound of my voice, Le Trépas turns. Blood trickles from his side, and from a wound on his right leg; my brother is a good shot. Still, there is a smile on his face, as though he can't feel the pain. Can he feel anything? He takes a step toward me, leaving a scarlet footprint behind him. "Did you think a bullet could stop me?" Le Trépas drags his fingers through his own blood. "Not even the old general made that mistake."

I take a breath, stepping back, staying out of reach. "I only wanted to know if the rumors are true," I call. "If you're really immortal."

"I told you once that I could give you the powers of the gods," the monk says, taking another step. "You didn't believe me."

"I believe you now," I say, letting fear creep into my voice. My eyes flick from his face to the open threat of his bloody hands. I need his blood for my plan to work—but I'm sure he wants mine too. "What do you want from me?"

"I want your help, of course," the monk says, as though the answer is obvious.

"To defeat the Aquitans?" I circle as I back away, trying not to get trapped against the curve of the bow.

"That's only the beginning," he replies, creeping

ever closer. The blood on his fingers gleams wetly in the torchlight. "Just imagine how powerful we could be. Life and death, hand in hand."

Life and death. What of knowledge? Know your enemy . . . I shake my head, trying to clear it. I have to focus. The monk is so close. I can read the tattoos that spill over his shoulders and down his bare arms: death, death, death, death. I have to be brave; I need that blood. So I plant my feet. "You want to work together?"

Reaching out, I take his hand, as if to shake it, Aquitan style, but he seizes my wrist so hard that my bones grind together. "In a manner of speaking," the monk hisses. "With my soul in your skin."

"What?" I can't help but recoil at his words, but his grip is too tight to escape. Under my fingers, his blood is warm, sticky. Frantically, I trace a mark on his wrist. I know he feels it. The monk quirks an eyebrow. Then he grins, drawing me close enough to whisper in my ear.

"Did you think your own blood could pull out my soul?" He draws a knife from his belt, the blade long and wicked. "I am not one of your puppets, child."

"I know," I say, my heart hammering in my chest as I twist in his grip. Does he mean to kill me here and now?

"The Keeper told me," I say, trying to stall. "I found the book in Aquitan. Forbidden magic. Stolen blood."

"So you know the spell?" Le Trépas cocks an eyebrow, the knife still high. "Life, death, and knowledge. And now, two of those gods will exist in one body," he adds. I cringe away, but his grip is too strong to break. "I always envied the power in the Maiden's blood."

"I didn't use my blood this time!" The blade shines in the moonlight, but as my words sink in, Le Trépas hesitates. Then he looks down at the symbol on his other wrist: not death, but life, traced out in his own red blood.

His eyes widen, and now he is the one to recoil. Releasing me, he drops the knife to scrub at the symbol. I stumble back out of reach, breathing hard. Will the magic work? Le Trépas seems to think so, but as I search the wide sky, there is no light but the moon. Then I see it, on the horizon—a blue glow, far away but speeding closer, faster than a falling star. Blue as a flame, blue as the ocean, blue as the heart of a sapphire. As I watch Le Trépas's soul returning, I suddenly know where he must have hidden it for so many years. The crown jewel had winked as I held it in my hands just hours ago. Before I had left it with Le Roi, just as Le Trépas had.

The monk follows my eyes, and the color leaves his face. "What did you do?"

"I gave you life," I say. "We've seen enough death, don't you think?"

The monk shows his teeth, his face ghastly in the light of his own spirit. Then he staggers backward as it pours into him like water into an empty vessel.

Le Trépas's back arches, taut as a violin string. Then he crumples like a page as the blue light fades, and blood pours afresh from his wounds. But he isn't dead—not yet. Slumped on the deck, he lifts his head to glare at me, his eyes a vengeful blue. Then he pushes himself to his feet, the knife still clenched in his fist.

"Kill her!" he shouts, and as one, the dead soldiers turn from the cabin door, their dead eyes fixed on me.

ACT 3,

SCENE 27

In the captain's cabin. LEO sits on the floor, his hands and feet bound once more, this time by AKRA. Now AKRA leans against the door, holding it shut against the dead outside. Suddenly, LE TRÉPAS's voice echoes across the deck.

LE TRÉPAS (*offstage*): Kill her!

The pounding stops, followed by a storm of trampling feet racing across the deck. AKRA sags against the door, breathing hard, but LEO's face goes white as he begins to tug at his bonds.

LEO: Akra? What's happening?
AKRA cracks open the door, peering outside.
AKRA: Le Trépas is on his knees. But the soldiers . . . she's going to be surrounded.
AKRA flings the door wide, but LEO's voice stops him before he can race to JETTA's aid.

LEO: Shoot him, Akra!

AKRA: What?

Shocked, AKRA turns to LEO, only to find him struggling against the already frayed ropes.

Leo—

LEO: He gave an order. I—ah!

Gritting his teeth, LEO pulls his hands free of the rope; fantouches are so strong. Fighting the command, his hands shake as he starts to undo the knots at his ankles. Still, AKRA hesitates, unsure whether to stop LEO or save JETTA as the soldiers close in.

Shoot him, please!

AKRA: It might not kill him.

LEO: You have to try.

AKRA: But it might kill *you*!

LEO: Better me than her!

As the ropes fall away, LEO pushes himself to his feet, stumbling toward the door. AKRA grabs him by the wrist, trying to hold him back with one hand. In the other, he raises his gun, aiming at LE TRÉPAS, but his eyes are on LEO's face.

> *LEO speaks slowly through his teeth.*

Shoot him. Save her.

From outside, JETTA's voice rings out.

JETTA: Akra!

Swearing, AKRA sights down the barrel and fires once, twice. Through the open door, he sees LE TRÉPAS stumble and fall, and the soldiers around him drop to the deck like the fruit of a poisoned tree.

Then AKRA turns, just in time to catch LEO as he too falls lifeless to the floor.

CHAPTER TWENTY-EIGHT

Le Trépas's soul is surprisingly bright.

It gleams on the deck, casting long shadows behind me. All around, other souls rise from the corpses of the soldiers, until the fading night glows bright as noon.

My body feels like it's floating too. I can't feel my feet. Is this what death feels like? But I am alive. It's hard to believe.

"Akra?" My brother is the one who saved me. Now he stumbles out of the cabin at my call. His face is a mask of relief—and something else. "Akra!"

"Jetta!" He's running toward me, his gun jammed in his belt. When he wraps his arms around me, he smells like sweat and blood and gunpowder, but he is undeniably alive as well. The comfort of that calms my racing heart, bringing me back to the ground. I don't know how long we stand that way, but when he finally pulls back, I can feel my feet again.

Then I look around the deck. "Where's Leo?"

My brother doesn't answer, so I look past him to the cabin. There, in the doorway, the golden light of another soul is gleaming.

My heart drops. I stumble closer, tripping over the bodies of the soldiers and falling to my knees. I try to get back up, but my legs are too unsteady, so I scramble closer on my hands. I can see his face long before I reach his side: Leo lying there, still, on the floor.

I sit back on my heels. The numb feeling has returned. It moves up my legs to my stomach, my heart, my head, swallowing me whole. Is this what death feels like? I thought I had survived, but now I'm not so certain.

"Jetta . . ." Akra's voice. He has followed me to the cabin, but I don't dare turn. I don't want to see him. "Le Trépas had already killed him by the time I got here. Are you . . . going to bring him back?"

My entire body tenses at the question. I look down at my bloody hands. I could do it. It wouldn't even hurt him.

With no wounds, there would be nothing to heal. Just a gentle ushering, a whispered word, an open door. The mark of life—like the one he wore on his shoulder. But I can't bring myself to answer my brother's question.

"Leave me alone," I say instead.

Akra hesitates—fighting the order—before he walks away.

He cannot disobey.

ACT 3,
SCENE 29

Dawn breaks over the Ruby Palace. Corpses litter the plaza—lying where they fell when LE TRÉPAS died. But as the griffin circles, THEODORA spies familiar faces below.

THEODORA: Camreon! Cheeky!

The two of them look up as THEODORA comes in for a landing. CHEEKY and TIA still wear their fine dresses, but CAMREON has changed into a pair of fine trousers and a white shirt. The outfit belonged to his brother, but the crown on his head was always supposed to be his.

Sliding from the griffin's back, THEODORA's legs shake as she races into CAMREON's arms. They hold each other tight as CHEEKY and TIA look on.

THEODORA: I'm so glad you're safe.

CHEEKY: Get a room.

TIA: They've got a whole palace.

THEODORA pulls back, looking around at the bodies, lying so still in the dawn light.

THEODORA: Is the palace . . . secure?

CAMREON: It is. From what I can see, Jetta found Le Trépas.

THEODORA nods.

There aren't many living soldiers left, but those who remain seem loyal to their paychecks. And I've sent word to my local contacts. They're gathering in the throne room.

THEODORA: And Raik?

CHEEKY interjects.

CHEEKY: Succumbed to his wounds.

CAMREON gives her a look, then puts his hand over his brow.

CAMREON: I'll tell you the whole story when there's more time. Is the *Prix de Guerre* safe?

THEODORA: I didn't stay to watch.

She hesitates, chewing her lip. Then she looks down to the book she holds.

Perhaps the Keeper can tell us how it ended.

CAMREON's eyes widen.

CAMREON: That's the Book of Knowledge?

In spite of herself, THEODORA smiles tightly.

THEODORA: It's been hidden in Aquitan for years. As soon as we're able, we can bring it back to the temple at

Kwai Goo. It takes ink rather than blood. Do you have a pen?

CAMREON: Inside. Come.

Leaving the griffin on the plaza, the rebels return to the palace to look for ink and answers. They do not like what they learn.

CHAPTER
THIRTY

It takes me some time to realize the boat is moving. When I do, I stand, feeling dizzy. Crossing the cabin, my feet feel like stones.

Passing through the doorway, I find a crowd on the deck. The Aquitans have emerged from below, hungry, tired, shivering from their ordeal—but they are alive.

There are souls here too, glimmering: the armée soldiers that Le Trépas had animated. Le Trépas's own soul must be somewhere among them. Should I find him? Trap him? Keep him from being reborn?

No—the Keeper had spoken of balance, and if a servant

exists for the Maiden, one must exist for the King. Besides, I won't live forever, and my death would free his soul if I trapped it. Better to let it go now, while I'm here to keep watch.

His body has been piled with the rest of them: the soldiers who had fallen, and the ones who had been thrown overboard to pull the ship. They'll be burned properly once we return to shore.

At some point, the ship had turned around. Now, we are close enough to Nokhor Khat that I can make out figures waiting at the dock. The crowd parts around me as I walk toward the bow. Akra is there, but he avoids my gaze, keeping his distance. A single long chain leads into the water. There is the dragon, toying with the swirling waves as she tows us into the harbor.

The Aquitans have clustered on deck, eager for the home they didn't know they loved so much. The spirits too have gathered, as though ready to embark for the temple. But to me, my own country seems a strange place. Unfamiliar. I have only been gone a few days, but everything has changed.

Camreon is waiting on the pier as the ship pulls in. At his back is a small force—a few palace guards and the local rebels he must have drummed up. As he welcomes the ship, I notice the dragon-bone crown on his head. I know I should feel relieved, but I don't feel much of anything.

His new armée ushers the refugees to the barracks for housing and medical care. The spirits disembark too, drifting toward Hell's Court in a river of gold. Only one stays behind: Leo's.

It stands over his body, as though keeping vigil alongside me. In the golden light of his soul, I try to read the song he left for me.

It scrawls across the floor: a rushed and careless carving, but no less beautiful than the stories chiseled into the stone of the temple. I run my hands over the marks; I can read the words, but the notes are harder. Papa and Maman were the musicians of our troupe. Still, I can make out the melody. It runs on a loop in my head.

When I hear the cabin door open, I don't bother looking up. "I told you to leave me alone."

"You told me no such thing." Cheeky—not Akra—is the one to reply, and her voice feels too harsh in the quiet cabin. "And how dare you think I'd listen?"

She barges in, Tia behind her, rushing to Leo's side to touch him, to hold him, to whisper his name. I can't bear the sight of their tears—the volume of their voices. Their open grief threatens the dull numbness I have wrapped around my heart, like a spark on a silk cocoon, with something tender and helpless writhing inside.

I turn away, but Theodora is hovering in the doorway, her face like a discarded page, crumpled and pale. Behind her, Camreon stands with his hand on her shoulder. Akra is behind them at a careful distance.

They all watch Leo—his final audience. But only I can see the bright light of his soul; the part that held his music and his jokes and the very essence of who he was. Why shouldn't I bring him back? My eyes go once more to the song he had written, and I know I can't.

I flex my empty hands. I feel like an outsider. Where is my power now? Going to the windows at the stern, I gulp fresh air as I stare out over the Hundred Days Sea. On the other side, Aquitan. I could go back. The king would have me if I groveled. There is very little that is familiar there, and nothing—no one—to remind me of what I'd lost here and now. I could live like Ayla did, my whole life a performance, my sins and secrets hidden away to everyone but me.

I am planning my escape when Tia starts to sing.

Her voice is richer with sorrow—like raw honey, like molten gold—and the sound of it washes everything else away. It is the song Leo wrote, but not the way it had looped through my head. It is not a dirge, but a love song.

Beside his body, his soul stirs. As Tia sings, I watch the golden light drift through the room, as though to greet all of us—or to say goodbye. And when he comes to me, I can almost feel the warmth of his arms, and the echo of his voice: au revoir.

"Au revoir," I whisper as Tia moves to the chorus, and Leo's spirit slips through the door and away toward the dock. Toward the temple. Toward his next life.

Theodora has seen me watching. "He's gone, isn't he?" she says softly, and with a start, I realize there are tears in my eyes.

Hurriedly, I dash them away. I could still call him back. I could. But I won't. Instead, I take a deep breath, looking around at the people he loved—the people who knew him best. "No," I say. "He's still here."

CHAPTER THIRTY-ONE

The last month of the rainy season passes in a blur.

Camreon has given me a fine room in the palace, with intricate mosaic floors and ivory inlay on golden teak panels, but after my time in Lephare, it's hard to see the beauty for the cost.

Luckily, Cam has always been a man of his word, and his coronation speech in Malao was not an empty promise. He and Theodora have started the endless work of tending the country.

They secure housing for the many refugees of the war—both Aquitan and Chakran alike. They bring the monks out of hiding to restore the temples and reopen the schools they used to run; Theodora even manages to let go of the Book of Knowledge, though I know she travels to the temple at Kwai Goo to consult the Keeper's monks as often as she can.

The sugar fields are returned to Chakran farmers in time for the planting season to start, and the largest plantation houses are made into hospitals and homes for the wounded and disabled. Some of the Aquitans had the nerve to object to this theft of their rightfully stolen wealth, but Camreon managed to wrangle funding from Le Roi Fou to pay them off.

He also managed to reopen trade at more favorable rates than before, and while I'm sure it had something to do with the Tiger's hard-headed negotiations, my own performance in Aquitan has certainly had an effect as well. Theodora and Camreon have gone back and forth a few times since, and she tells me that my skeletal fantouches have permeated local superstition—a threat for misbehaving children, or a curse bandied about between their elders.

Le Roi sent the fantouches themselves back aboard the ship he'd promised, and we'd sent the ship back to Lephare carrying quite a few living Aquitans. But others chose to stay, swearing fealty to the new king in their new home. The skeletal fantouches themselves have become part of

Camreon's palace guard—loyal and tireless, and a reminder of the link between the throne and the temples.

This news makes me smile, but not for long. I myself have made no new fantouches since then. My friends have come by with supplies—leather and paint and wood, bamboo and brass and brushes—to try to keep me occupied. Cheeky and Tia keep insisting that I need to put on a show at their new theater; Camreon has given them the Royal Opera House to run, although to hear Cheeky tell, she does most of the legwork while Tia spends every spare hour at the inn. Apparently the innkeeper's eldest daughter is quite taken with her.

But both Cheeky and Tia have told me they want Chakran performances for their opening season. So far, they have commitments from many of the troupes returning from Aquitan, including the Ros Sook. But I have no inspiration. When I pick up a piece of leather or a strand of ribbon, my hands feel numb, and my mind is dark as an unlit stage.

Most days, I sit at the polished ebony table by my window, Leo's violin case open before me. Cheeky and Tia brought it to me weeks ago, and I like to look at the sheet music inside. He had written many other songs, just as his own mother had. I had even heard him play them from time to time, never knowing they were his own. But when I hold the sheet music and close my eyes . . . sometimes I swear I can still hear the sound of his violin.

I am listening to it when a knock at the door shakes the notes out of my head. Is it lunch already? I have half a mind to ignore whoever is there, but the last time I did, Theodora barged in anyway. My friends are determined to keep after me—though in recent weeks, their constant company has eased into more manageable visits at mealtimes, and instead of trying to get me to come out of my room, they mostly just make sure I'm eating.

Still, I am annoyed at the interruption. Tucking the music back in the case, I stomp across the room and swing the door open. The sudden brightness of the hall makes me wince. Maman is there, her hand raised to knock again. Papa is just behind her, with my brother pushing his chair. And when Maman wraps me up in a tight hug, I realize how long it's been since I've seen my family.

After a moment, I lean into her embrace. Then I reach over her shoulder to hold Papa's hand. But Akra doesn't so much as look at me—still under orders. "Come in," I say, suddenly sheepish. Stepping back, I lead them all through the door. "Please."

"You promised to write," Maman says pointedly, peering around the room at the rumpled bed, the half-filled cups, the clothes scattered across the floor

"I'm sorry," I say. "I've been busy."

"I can tell." She starts to pick things up, and it makes me feel like a child again. I turn to the bed, straightening my rumpled sheets, but it feels like I'm moving through molasses. Then I feel a gentle hand on my arm. "Let me take care of it," Maman says, drawing me back to my chair. As I sit, she opens the shutters. Daylight spills in, brighter than a soul. "Sometimes it's hard to realize how deep the shadows have gotten until someone else points them out."

"We're worried about you," Papa says as Maman returns to her cleaning. Despite the slurred sounds of his speech, I have spent enough time listening to him to know what he is saying. "Have you been taking your elixir?"

"I have," I say, nodding to the flask on the dresser; by the time the supply from Le Roi had run low, Theodora had found the stockpile Le Trépas had brought to Hell's Court. "There are some things medicine can't fix."

"Moping doesn't help much, either," Akra says as he comes to my side. "The show must go on."

I glare up at him, but the expression on his face quenches the brief spark of my anger. He rests a gentle hand on the violin case, and I remember that his own death had been to save Leo. But after a moment, he pushes the violin gently aside, making room for the bag he's carrying. When he drops the sack on the table, it moves.

"What's this?" I say, but before he can answer, a familiar fantouche bounds from the sack, then falls right off the edge of the table. "Miu!"

Rolling to her feet, the dragon fantouche lifts her chin as though daring me to laugh. Then she twitches her tail and leaps into my lap, butting her head up under my hand. "Fine leatherwork on that one," Papa says softly, nodding at Miu. "But the handling could be better."

"We'll need quite a few more fantouches if we're to rebuild our collection in time," my brother adds.

"In time for what?" I say, stroking Miu's leather horns.

"For the performance at the Royal Opera House," Maman says as she makes the bed. Miu leaps down from my lap to slip underneath the sheet, and I frown.

"Who said anything about performing at the Royal Opera House?"

"Cheeky did," my brother says. "And if you think

your orders are hard to disobey, you've never seen the consequences she can mete out."

"We heard about your solo performance in Aquitan," Maman says over her shoulder. "Are you too good for your troupe these days?"

"The Shepherd and the Tiger," Papa adds, a wistful look in his eyes. "I would have loved to see your version."

"I think the next one will be even better," Akra says, pulling something else out of the bag. "We still need a tiger, but I made a new shepherd."

The fantouche he holds is almost as tall as he is, with graceful jointing and finely scraped leather. I can see the care and the time Akra must have put into it—he was always a better artist than me. But it is not the pains he has taken that give me pause, but the appearance of the fantouche itself.

In the story, the shepherd carries a staff, but this one holds a pen, and instead of a sarong, he wears a linen suit. But the face itself is new and familiar all at once—the features unmistakably Leo's. "It's . . . beautiful work," I say at last.

"It was *a lot* of work," Akra replies, laying the fantouche down gently over the back of another chair. "But there's still more work to do."

He turns to the pile of supplies Cheeky brought me. Leather and silk, paper and paint. . . . Picking up the shears and a roll of leather, my brother sets them before me on the table, but I look out through the open window over the city below.

The streets are full of souls, both living and dead. A line of monks winds through them on their way back to Hell's Court from the market near the docks. There are ships in the harbor—trading ships—from Aquitan and the Lion Lands, and the doors at Le Livre are open to visitors.

If I lean out a little farther, I can see the Royal Opera House, and I can imagine the empty space on the marquee. The show must go on. Life must go on, even though death is a part of it. And there is still so much to tell of all that happens in between.

Turning back to my brother—to my family—I pick up the tools they have given me and set to work.

TONIGHT!
TONIGHT! TONIGHT!

At the
Royal Opera House
in Nokhor Khat

THE ROS NAI

WILL PRESENT

THE
SHEPHERD
AND
THE TIGER

AUTHOR'S NOTE

When I set out to write a series with a bipolar main character, I didn't realize how my own mental health would affect the actual writing process. It seems silly in retrospect, but I had assumed I would be studying my own madness through a glass—observing and recording from the outside.

Surprise—the glass was a mirror all along.

However, it's worthwhile to note that some of the ways that I have written "malheur" will not always align with the experiences of everyone with bipolar disorder. (They don't always align exactly with my own, either.) Rather, I have used my reality to inspire the story—though I have stuck more closely to reality when it comes to bipolar than I have in, say, my references to history, technology, or language.

Still, while this is a work of fiction, the heart of this story is strong and true: art is a powerful weapon, and love is our best defense.

ACKNOWLEDGMENTS

Writing a series can sometimes feel like a fight, and battles are never waged on a single front.

In the hard-won victory of the final book in a three-book series, my editor Martha Mihalick has been the most capable general I could imagine. I would follow her anywhere.

My agent Molly Ker Hawn is an expert quartermaster. It's thanks to her that I know what I'm doing, and when, and what to expect when I get there.

Thanks also to Mike Pettry, my old buddy in the writerly trenches, and to the team at Greenwillow, who ride quickly and boldly forward into new territory.

Speaking of ride or die, I'm forever grateful to my husband, Bret Heilig, and for our kids, one who speaks softly and the other who carries a big stick.

And now that the battle is through, I'd like to thank my readers most of all, for believing in the justness of the cause.